Maid for My Billionaire Boss

J.P. Sterling

Maid for My Billionaire Boss

Editors: Lawrence Editing and Barren Acres Editing

Proofreader: Samantha Pottie

This is a work of fiction. Any mention of names, places, and characters is fiction and for entertainment purposes only.

Contents

One

Atalie

"Your résumé is almost blank, Ms. Pearson." The woman who identified herself as *the* Mrs. Michael peered over her on-trend glasses while she held my paper like it was an annoying utility bill. I marveled at the way her hair layered in puffed curls, overlapping like a perfectly plotted patchwork quilt on the top of her head. She definitely had her own ozone hole trailing behind her like a sluggish halo from the amount of product she had used to shellac her hair helmet in place. "Forgive me for being so blunt, but what do you do for money?"

My voice snagged in the back of my throat, which astonished me because I had never found a word I didn't love to express. However, I still didn't know how to explain to myself the recent oddities of my life. When I didn't respond, she lowered her brows, and continued, "My apologies. That was terribly rude, but I'm trying to get an understanding of what skills you have."

"I thought it was an entry-level job." I managed in a reluctant defense because the truth of why my résumé was blank was far too impossible to explain. Worse than trying to explain differential equations, and it's not even like I knew what those were.

"Well, it is, but it isn't." She set my résumé d own on her desk. "Cleaning isn't hard, but Trey does have many valuable items in the home—in addition to a rare art collection—so I need character references." She rotated her swivel chair square with my own. "You want to work for one of the richest men in the city and gave me nothing about your life. No people to call or businesses to reference. This doesn't give me much to go on for such a delicate job posting."

I deadpanned, wondering how a simple job interview could make me feel like I'd broken a law. "I assure you, ma'am, that is all I have."

Motioning to the stack of papers next to her, she went on, "I've had so many applicants for this job that I could never interview them all, but I can sort them into two piles." She flipped one over and read, "College student. Fashion major. No jobs. Hobbies: going to the beach." She flicked her eyes back to mine. "She's not applying for a job to clean a house if you know what I mean." She reached out in the most graceful manner until her arm hovered over the trash can and gingerly dropped the résumé.

Then she returned to the résumé pile and grabbed the next one. "Thirty years of experience in house management and a full list of references. Mom of five. Grandmother of three." A pleased grin spread on her face, and she neatly set that résumé back in the pile. "She sounds lovely, and I'll have to call her."

Retrieving my résumé, she flashed it at me. In a voice so hushed it hinted at an enchantment like a narrator of a children's storybook, she said, "There's a story here you aren't telling me." She crossed her arms loosely in front of her on the surface of her desk and leaned forward in anticipation.

I let out a secret groan, then grimaced when my secret groan hadn't exactly been a silent one. My eyes skirted the room, pining for the exit. At this point, she obviously wasn't giving me the job, which grated my nerves because I really needed money—*yesterday!* With only thirty-seven bucks left in my bank account— add to that the way she looked at me—I panicked and blurted out, "I was married." My words came out all on top of one another, making my reply sound like a single, long word.

She tilted her head a-hungry-for-details measure. "Divorced?"

My heart wildly revolted at the mere suggestion of my departed love divorcing me. An illegal interview question on so many levels, but everything about her told me she wasn't afraid to get personal. I wasn't trying to be secretive, and I was aware of how shady a blank application looked. I was one of those people who had life experience and not job experience. I didn't know how to put School of Hard Knocks on paper. Hiding my gaze in the shield of my lap, I replied, "No, ma'am. He passed last year. We managed an art studio together. If you're worried about the art collection, it would be in good hands with me."

"I'm sorry about your loss." Her voice was small but not quiet. In an odd way, I felt like she was confirming something she had already guessed. "So, it's just you?"

"I have a son." Blindsided by how hard this felt to say, I forced myself to bravely let my eyes hit hers again. "He's eight and, to be honest . . ." I sucked in a deep breath as I felt my eyes start to sting. "I applied for this position because I was hoping I could bring him with me to work. He's no trouble. I promise you won't even notice him. If anything, I'll get done faster because he's a big help."

Her lips pinched in an untelling way before she reached her arm forward, offering a handshake, and said, "You're hired."

My head jolted. "I-I am?"

A spark of victory twinkled in her eye before she spoke in her enchanted narrator voice, "Years ago, I was a single mom who had to start over with a résumé exactly like this one." Her lips curled into a coy smile. "I knew there was a story here. Forgive me if that seemed derogatory, but I didn't think I could pass your application up if I hadn't known the truth."

I blinked back a tear and quietly nodded, unable to add anything about this uncanny coincidence.

Mrs. Michael switched back to her business tone, pulled out another sheet of paper, and slid it across the desk to me. "This is our nondisclosure agreement. Before I can proceed with telling you about the job and salary, and giving you a tour of the home, I need you to sign on the Xs." She slid her French-manicured finger to the first line. She held a pen out to me with her free hand. I had wanted to ask some questions, but the way she hovered her finger on the X told me I wasn't allowed to ask any until after I'd signed the confidentiality agreement. I obediently took the pen and signed on all the lines and set her pen neatly next to the sheet.

"Wonderful." As soon as the word was out of her mouth, she snatched the sheet and dropped it into a file folder. As she stood, she said, "I'll give you a tour of the house now."

She led the way out of her office down the hall, her heels clicking on the wood floors. "This week Trey is in the process of closing his West Coast office but starting next week, he will be working out of his home office full time. To start, you can work full time since the home has been empty for so long and needs more care. Once the home is up to shape, you only need to come as needed but the salary will stay the same." Stopping in front of a room at the end of the hall, she turned back to me as she pushed the door open. "This is his private office. You should try your best to clean it regularly, and I would prefer you start in here first thing Monday."

I followed her inside what seemed like a modest office. I could tell by the bare shelves lining the wall, he hardly spent time here. Mrs. Michael ran her hand along one of the shelves, adding a film to her finger. Giving me a wrinkled nose grin, she firmly stated. "This needs a good scrub." She retrieved a tissue from a nearby box, wiped her finger off, and tossed it into the trash can. When she turned back to me, the only photo on the shelf caught her eye. "Oh, here's a photo of Trey and me." She grabbed it, flashing it in my direction. "You can at least see what he looks like since you can't meet him today."

Glancing in the direction of the frame, I expected to see a man who matched her in poise. The face smiling back at me was young—obviously physically fit and demurely handsome. I immediately assumed Mrs. Michael must have been the one to bring money into their marriage because there was no way this arrangement would work any other way. She was still beaming back at me, holding the frame like she was expecting me to comment. I closed my stunned jaw. "Uh, lovely couple."

"Excuse me?" Her brow flattened. "Trey is my son."

My mouth made a silent oh, while I sucked in an extra breath, and wondered how I was going to take my clumsy foot out of my mouth. Deciding flattery was prime, I was about to tell her there was no way that a grown man could ever be her son because she didn't look a day over thirty-five, but she broke the silence by inserting her own laughter, and said, "Oh my." She pressed a flattened palm against her chest. "Pardon me for not being clearer. I had assumed you knew who Trey was. Many of the applicants applied simply because they wanted to meet him. That's why I did the interviews for him." She put the frame back on the shelf, and with a smile still dimpling her cheek, she asked, "You must not be from around here, are you?"

"No, I relocated last week."

"Welcome to the area." Her eyes steadied on me in a way that was more piercing than comfortable. "What brings you here?"

Before I could hold back, I found my words escaping. "I inherited my mother-in-law's house here on Long Island. I wanted to . . ." *Breathe again* is what I felt like saying, but I didn't want to get *that* personal. *Nor did I want to tell her I had been homeless.* I wagged my head, trying to fill in my broken words with something. "Try something different. I'll admit we've had a hard year, but now we're ready for an adventure."

"That sounds lovely, and having been in your situation before, I would have to agree that you are doing the right thing." Her words were soft and warm, like everybody's favorite Southern grandma. Then she put on a polite smile, walking forward. "Let's get back to the tour. So, you may think this house is modest for a man like Trey. This is the home he grew up in, and I've long since moved into a new condo. However, Trey has always held on to it because of the sentimental elements." She chatted as she strolled through the long hall. I was eager to get over the personal talk, so I willingly followed her through all the nooks of the home.

We reached the end of the upstairs hall, where the natural lighting dimmed, and the ceiling caved into a low slant, creating a little nook. A tiny wooden door—the size of half of a person—perched out of the nook. It looked so quaint that it grabbed my attention. Having done a thorough walkthrough of each room up until this point, where she took great care to tell me each thing I was—and was not—allowed to touch, I figured she'd take me inside the tiny room. However, she breezed right past it. Not wanting to overlook something that would be my responsibility, I slowed my steps. "Do I need to take care of this room?"

She turned around in what appeared to be a slow-motion setting. "Oh, that's the attic." I could tell she was forcing a breezy tone, but her eyes bore a tinge of worry, betraying her. "Actually, that room is private."

My mind flashed to beautiful maidens locked in a round tower and secret children on a diet of rat-poisoned cookies. I was about to scoff at myself for being foolish and blame the secrecy of the attic on it being full of disorganized junk she didn't want me to see, but just as I smiled at her, ready to agree, her eyes narrowed, and her face paled.

"Are you okay?" I asked her, concerned.

"Most definitely." Her voice was too firm to be believable and her eyes still steadied on the little door before finally whisking them back to me. "I'm sure we won't have any issues with anything, will we?"

"I-I, ah, no. Don't think so . . ." My voice trailed off as I had a budding seed of anxiety over what I had gotten into.

Two

Atalie

I wasn't nervous, per se, about my first day of work, even though I had no professional experience with keeping a house clean, other than my own. The entirety of my training could be credited to the many hours of reruns I had watched of *The Brady Bunch. I was a huge Alice fan.* She never had a hair out of place, her clothes were never wrinkled, and the kitchen was always spotless. With her as my role model, I tied my long ebony hair back into a low ponytail and found a cute black house dress to slip on for fun. Well, if I were being honest, I would have to call it a smock because I had used it for our preschool painting classes at the art studio. Since I no longer had a need—nor the means—to teach little humans, I found it frugal to rebrand my wardrobe.

I was on my third lap of nervously pacing the living room—well, not nervously, more like methodically—when Josiah peeked his head out from behind his bedroom door, fully dressed for the day. I called up to him while he stood at the top of the stairs. "How'd you sleep?"

He lifted his shoulders, telling me he hadn't. Having never been much of a deep sleeper to begin with, he'd always had a brain like a motor, one that only accelerated faster with his thoughts the moment he lay down. His father had always teasingly blamed it on me, saying he took after me. Ever since the move, his constant thoughts seemed to ebb even faster. Recently though, he had learned to keep them hushed—which in a way was a relief because I didn't have to listen to his unfiltered ramblings—but it often left him silent, where he'd stare blankly and shrug at me.

"Are you hungry?"

He descended the stairs, but another shrug told me it was too early for him to eat. I was sort of feeling the same. Well, too early and too nervous to eat. His cryptic expression left me confused. Since he obviously didn't want to eat, I didn't know what to do with the extra time. I funneled my excess energy into finger snaps I popped as I swung my hands in front of me like a tone-deaf conductor who couldn't find the beat. A thought popped into my head: "Let's just leave now. We can take the long way and walk along the beach."

His eyes widened, glittering back at me and I took that as a yes. A moment later we were out the door, headed east along the shoreline. It hadn't been my decision to live on the beach, but since we were here in the house my husband grew up in, I loved it immensely. I found the ambiance of the waves, along with the rhythmic movement, to be intoxicating and truly one of the only things able to drown out my sensory overload. *Serenity.*

Josiah skirted along the water's edge, fearlessly letting the tide roll over his bare toes as he carried his sandals in one hand and picked up rocks with his other. Being a hobbyist in skipping stones, he had honed an eye for finding the flattest rocks. He tossed them back over the early dawn reflective water, counting the bounces out loud, and cheered fiercely when they went over four jumps.

Since it wasn't too far out of the way, we took our time crossing the beach. I drank in the salty air, feeling it tranquilize the quibbles in my gut. By the time we reached the house, the sun was cresting the street enough to tell the lampposts it was their turn to sleep. I let us into the grand front entrance with the key Mrs. Michael had given me. One look at the empty and too-cool-to-be-comfortable foyer sent a new wave of jitters to meet my fingers. "New adventure day one," I whispered.

Josiah followed me as I moved to the kitchen. My shoulder blades stiffen as the marble floors looked cold and uninviting and I made a conscious decision to keep my Alice-inspired sneakers on. Josiah matched my tone when he asked, "Why are we whispering?"

My eyes skirted down the hall, but I held my head steady, like a spy. "It feels like a secret."

"Mom, you're being weird."

I cracked a smile and reached my hand out to ruffle the top of his sea-crusted hair. "Is that your final assessment, wise Mr. Chewbacca?"

"First of all, it's not mister. Let's get that straight. Plus, Chewbacca isn't the smart one." He rolled his eyes while he headed to the kitchen table. I took a second to reflect on my Star Wars knowledge as it wasn't something I had grown up with, but a recent affection of Josiah's that I was happy to indulge in. Apparently, I needed to watch it again. "It was Yoda, right?" I spoke to his back. "Chewbacca is the hairy one."

"It's okay if it's over your head." He pointed to the high-top table in the kitchen. "Can I set my stuff here?" Without waiting for a reply, he let the tie-dyed backpack he had made with his dad slide down his bony shoulder and he sat at one of the high-back stools.

"I think that's a perfect spot," I called as I stuck my head into the broom closet. I scanned the domestic tools in front of me, getting acquainted with the layout. Before I lost my nerve and ran home, I grabbed a hand duster and secured the Hoover in my other hand, dragging it along behind me. Then I called back, "Mrs. Michael wanted me to start in the office, so I'll be down the hall." I motioned with my duster like I was directing an airplane, but Josiah was already face down in his homework, missing my grandiose gestures entirely.

Padding down the hall, I slowed my stride before I got to the office to listen for human activity. The door to Mr. Michael's office was ajar and the lights were on like he had recently been there. I timidly stuck my head in and found it empty, so I took that as my invitation to enter.

I had no idea if there was a proper way to go about maiding around. The empty bookshelf seemed like a good place to start. I used my duster to mop up the accumulated dirt. It only took a moment, and I felt a tickle in my nose, but I flexed my face a few times to wiggle it out. *This isn't so bad.*

I moved to the next shelf and picked up my pace as I swept my duster along the mahogany wood. "*Ol' Alice don't have nothin' on me,*" I mused out loud in my latest impression of a New Jersey character accent. In no time, I had cleared the shelves, which seeded my confidence and I set my eyes on the desk.

It was one of those huge obtrusive ones you see in the movies when they show rich people in their offices. I found it comical he would need a desk that large because the only thing on it was an open laptop centered in front of his chair and a reusable coffee mug. It was rather boring when I assessed it. It made me think back to my husband's desk which I had cleaned many times. Having been an artist, his desk was always messy and vibrant—full of ideas . . . and life. No matter how hard I tried to clean it, it would never wipe clean as the remnants of his latest masterpiece would stain like a blueprint.

Visualizing the montage I had loved, my eyelids drifted down. I knew better than to dwell on it though, because it would bring the sting in my eyes. I moved quickly—too quickly toward the desk and my legs became entangled with a cord. My eyes immediately darted to the floor, but then alerted back to the desk when the laptop rocketed across it, hooking the coffee mug in its cord. The cup spilled like July wildfires all over the keyboard before it finally claimed the computer as a hostage and tossed it screen down on the floor!

My hand slapped my mouth, suppressing a scream! Still entangled in the cord, I didn't care as I panicked and reached to rescue the computer, praying it would be okay. Then I realized I had been foolish for not caring

I was still tangled because I tripped again! If I had been an oaf at the top of this sequence, suddenly I was a ninja and I caught myself by dropping to my knee, and that was swift, so I smiled. Until I heard the vacuum switch on which perplexed me . . . I felt tugging on my ponytail—it was light at first but grew in intensity. Turning cautiously—I freaked! The noise I had credited to the vacuum—wasn't the vacuum at all! The end of my ponytail was disappearing into a nearby paper shredder. I yanked back, trying to free my hair, but it hurt as it only pulled me closer, chewing my hair—my perfect hair that took me four years to grow this long. I cried out, "Help!" with every puff of air I could muster out of my lungs as the lifeline of hair between me and the beast of the shredder was getting shorter.

This shredder was not an average shredder! It seemed to be on some sort of a workout program because it motored like a speedboat. It chewed, revving even louder, taunting me by drowning out my cries for help. I rapidly switched the settings button, but no matter what I did, the thing wouldn't reverse. I must have jammed it or maybe it was possessed. I had a revelation. *Unplug it!* I reached around the girth of the basket and gripped it firmly. Not wasting a second to find the cord, I yanked until I felt a release—a sweet release, quieting the motor.

I panted, letting my fear subside and my eyes started to waver, feeling dizzy. No, hungry because I hadn't eaten breakfast—or both. I was woozy and drunk on adrenaline and holding this paper shredder was heavier than one would think. I needed to sit. I clenched the shredder basket close to my head to prevent it from pulling my hair as it still owned me in its claw. I hobbled to the chair, but I heard a shuffle from the door, and my eyes skirted to meet it. The handsome man from the photo was standing before me. Trey was here! He didn't waste time loitering in the doorway, gawking at me, but instead, he took long steps into the room.

His eyes held a fiery irritation and were fixed on me when he demanded, "What's going on?"

I gritted my teeth, while still coddling the shredder next to my head. *This is not the way I planned on impressing my boss today!* "Please don't fire me!" I blurted out. "Um, I mean, hello. I'm the new housekeeper and I was cleaning your desk. I seemed to have gotten sucked into the paper shredder. I'm okay, though . . ." My voice trailed off because he had rounded the corner and caught sight of his computer still marinating in a puddle of coffee. His eyes fled back to me, but before he could yell at me, I added, "Sorry, I tripped, and it slipped."

If this had been a cartoon, his eyes would have glowed crimson, and black steam would have jetted out of his ears. I placed one timid foot in front of the other, waiting for my invisible powers to kick in as I set my sight on the exit. *I'm getting fired, and I have no money. I'm going to have to literally beg on the street for money to feed my son, which may take some time. I might as well just see myself out now so I can get started on that.*

Surprisingly, he didn't yell. Instead, he asked in a calm voice, "Where are you going?"

I'd always been petite and had to stand on my toes to reach any closet shelf, but I'd never felt more freakishly teeny in my life when I looked back at him. "Er, I thought you were mad, so I was going to get out of your way."

"I'm not happy, but I might also be concerned there's a strange woman in my office wearing my paper shredder as a hat." He had one of those voices that was a bit raspy, like he was on the verge of getting a cold. Then he motioned to his paper shredder still embedded in my hair. I clenched it like it was a security object I could hide behind when he said, "I can at least let you out of that thing before you go." His lips curled a tiny bit but strained like he was holding back laughter. "Unless you want to walk around like that?"

My shoulders dropped some of the weight of embarrassment at the hint of his sense of humor, and I breathed a heavy sigh of relief. "Please." I took a step closer to him, adding, "I tried to pull my hair out, but it won't reverse at all."

He dug into his top drawer for a pair of scissors. "That might be because I got the industrial-grade shredder," he mused, the ends of his lips teasing a smile.

Still thinking it was insane for needing a shredder with a five-hundred-horse-power motor, I was too flustered to think of anything intelligent to add, so I tried to infuse humor into the situation by sarcastically saying, "Well, thanks for that."

"You're welcome." He motioned to his chair with the point of his scissors, his eyes dropping to mine. "You must be Atalie?"

Now that I was standing this close to him, I could see his eyes were blue, but not like Josiah's. More like a rare shade of indigo, making me wonder if maybe they were contacts because it was such a unique hue. "I am," I answered in a small voice, "and in case you're wondering, I'm not always this impressive." I quirked one side of my lips and sank down onto his chair, perching on the edge like an astute student. I paused my breath when I noticed he was cute, like make-my-knees-shake-being-so-close handsome. He was standing closer than a casual dance partner and my head was parallel with his chest—only inches from it, which made it incredibly hard not to stare at. He was moderately tall. Actually, he was the perfect size I could fit right under his chin. *Not that I thought about anything like that*!

My cheeks raged in humiliation when he poked the tip of the scissors under my hair. I was grateful he was focused on my head and couldn't see my cheeks light up like a glow bug. This was clearly the junior-high experience I had never had. I sucked in a loud breath when I heard the first snip.

He quickly retreated his scissors, peering down at me. "Are you okay?"

"In what sense are you asking?"

"In the sense that I didn't *stab* you."

"Nope, in that way, I'm still doing quite well." I started to let out a nervous giggle when he went in for another cut. I stiffened until the tension on my hair released and I was free.

He took the shredder from me. My eyes followed the basket until he set it on the desk, and I gasped when I saw several inches of my hair still stuck in its claw! "My hair!" One hand flew forward, longing for the hair I had lost, but my other hand fled to my head, trying to cover the part that had been scalped. I didn't even dare sneak a peek at how bad I looked because the mortification would have slayed me. I wasn't what you would call vain, but any normal person would have been feeling over-exposed in this situation. I pulled my lips into a squeamish smile as I fumbled for the words to make my shame go away. "Thanks, and sorry . . ."

"It's okay." His face held a soft expression, but his eyes stole a look at his laptop on life support on the floor.

"I can replace it," I blurted out and leaned forward to pick it off the floor. When I lifted it, a trail of coffee beaded down from the corner, making us both cringe and again, I fumbled. "It totally hurts to be this talented." Then I sputtered out a nervous chuckle—something I didn't think I would be capable of—but it was either give into the mortification or cry.

His eyes held a twinkle of amusement when he reached forward, taking the computer from me. Before I could apologize again, he reassured me, "You're lucky because it's a new computer and I didn't have anything important on it yet." Motioning to the box on the floor, he tacked on, "I was unpacking it to set it up."

I gnawed on my lip while we both stared at the stream of coffee that was still running like the last random drips in a perfectly pressed shot of espresso. "I can clean it up," I offered in a response that seemed to hang in the air long after I spoke.

He held up his hand in a firm stop. "Nah, I think you've done enough here. Maybe you can stick to the kitchen?"

Motioning my head toward the door that never looked more inviting, I murmured, “Right. Um, I can leave now.” I took eager steps toward the exit and called back over my shoulder, “Um, sorry.”

“It’s okay.” I heard his reply, but I was too chicken to glance back at him. I sped away like I had the fullest of bladders, knowing full well today was going to be one of those days I would always remember with a cringe on my face.

THREE

Trey

I sat in my office holding what was left of my new maid's ponytail. She had left my office to clean—or do whatever she called what she was doing—in my kitchen. She had looked embarrassed enough that I didn't think I needed to add fuel to it by trying to talk. The whole circumstance was odd, as I wasn't ever one of those people who understood what to do in emergency situations involving people. Give me software viruses, tech malfunctions, and anything relying on a black-and-white science to solve, but people—especially those of the female sort—usually succeeded in confusing me.

Okay, maybe disabling would be a better word.

Yep. Complete system malfunction.

I held her hair, wondering if this was something she would have wanted back. Tonya was on her way over and I wasn't sure why, but I felt having a random female's ponytail in my office would be one of those things which fell into the "hard to explain to your girlfriend category." I panicked and dropped the hair like it was a hot potato into the trash can.

I picked up my phone and called Evan because even though I had texted him an hour ago, he hadn't gotten back to me. Evan was a buddy of mine

I'd had since college. We had shared the same major, as well as dorm room. Also, he'd never admit to it, but I suspected we might have also shared a girlfriend. My evidence was when I tripped over a pair of pink skater shoes on the front doormat one night when I came home a day early from break. Pink shoes weren't his style, and there was only one girl I'd ever seen who wore them. *The girl I was casually dating*. It's fine, though, and she wasn't my type. We literally had only dated a couple weeks while Tonya and I had taken a break. I mostly dated her to make Tonya jealous—which worked because we quickly got back together.

Now Evan had his own computer shop and he stayed only busy enough to be able to close by noon every day so he could go to the beach. He seemed to live life as one big party, void of responsibility. And almost like he did it to cement the stereotype even more, yes, he still lived at home with his mom. Even though I became rich, he remained my closest friend because he's the only one who really knew me before I had my tech company—well, besides Tonya and Damion. Evan answered on the first ring with the nickname we always called each other: "Amateur."

"Why don't you make yourself useful and send me over another laptop?" I greeted him.

"Useful people get used." His voice rolled out in a smooth tone. "I prefer to be beneficial."

"I don't want to hear about your benefits."

"So," he started in a curious tone. "What happened to the computer you just picked up?"

"My new maid dropkicked it to the floor and poured coffee all over it."

"Maid. Is that code?"

"No, it's not code."

"Is she hot?"

"I only got to look at her scalp, but it looked healthy. I didn't see any flakes or fungus or anything if that's your standard."

"And . . . Why exactly were you looking at her scalp?"

"Evan," I stated firmly, redirecting his focus. "Computer."

"You're super rich. How come you don't have dozens of fancy prototypes in your office?"

"Well, because I just moved here and because you're my computer guy. You don't give me fancy prototypes. So, computer."

"Don't rush me. I need to make sure I'm getting something fair out of this deal."

"Since I'm your only customer, my loyalty should be enough."

"Funny guy, better watch it or I'll make your laptop run slower than a 1997 Presario with a 56k modem."

I chuckled because I remembered that piece of junk. My first computer and it only took me four paper routes to afford it. Keeping with the serious tone of this conversation, he added, "Would you like me to bill you for the extended warranty on our friendship or do you want to pay over the phone?"

"What?"

"This abuse is starting to be too much. I'm going to have to charge you."

I didn't respond because I heard Tonya's sultry voice at the door. "Trey."

Waving her inside, I spoke back into my phone, "Same computer as last time, but I have to go." Ending my call, I turned to greet her. The smile I was beginning to etch on my face from the sound of her voice was instantly diminished when I saw her expression. "What's wrong?" I asked, walking to meet her, but instead of embracing her, I stopped an arm's length away.

"I got your message about the dinner reservations for tomorrow night." Her tone was edged in a way that irritated my ears, tipping me off that she was unhappy.

"I made reservations at your favorite restaurant for ten of your closest friends and family so we could celebrate your birthday."

"It's not my favorite restaurant," she quipped with a hand perched on her hip in a manner which made me want to take a step back. "But it is a place I enjoy. You know my favorite place is in LA."

"Right." I closed my mouth, trying to maintain an indifferent look. When the truth was, we both knew her frustration had nothing to do with the restaurant at all. She was growing bitter over my choice to move back to the East Coast. We were both from Long Island—high school sweethearts. She had always spoken dreamily of moving to the West Coast. I never wanted to stand in the way of her dreams. She had been the sole reason I had moved my offices there in the first place, even though I never wanted to leave my friends and family.

I tried it *for her*. I'd try anything for her, and I don't regret it.

However, this last year my life had taken an unexpected tremendous downhill slide where I almost lost everything. Almost losing everything is a *bit* of an understatement. My business partner died, my business lost millions, my employees backstabbed me, and I ended up on the brink of a total nervous breakdown. It was either check into a psych ward and wait to die or start over.

Now my goal was to get a fresh start with people I *trusted*, my way back to sanity was to be closer to my inner circle—the people who knew me before I was rich. I was surprised she made the move back with me. I thought for sure she would use the move as a reason to break up, but somehow, she managed to leave her life there.

I was grateful for that.

However, it seemed no matter what I did to smooth the transition, she was headstrong about making us both miserable. I was beginning to think our mutual love for each other wasn't going to be enough, and maybe we needed to admit we'd grown into different people. I still cared about her though. I wasn't the sort of guy who blew through relationships, and I also wasn't going to add any fuel to her issue, so I blankly stared back at her.

"I'm confused," she went on in a little softer tone, but the expression she held revealed she wasn't at all confused. "I had wanted to spend the weekend in LA with my friends. I don't understand why you made reservations here."

"We already talked about this. Remember? I can't get away this weekend because my business partners are coming. Once I get through the next couple of weeks, we can take off for a whole week if you want."

She pushed her bottom lip out in a way I used to think was cute, but lately I'd been seeing so much of it, I started to get defensive every time I saw it.

Not today.

I turned, heading back to my desk. "Let's not fight about this. How about we grab a coffee?" I offered since the one I had made ended up watering my hardware.

"I want to go to LA."

Disappointed about the direction of this conversation, I also wasn't shy about holding her eyes when I frankly stated, "You can go if you want, but I can't get away."

"What's the catch?"

Her lips curled at me from across the room, but I stubbornly didn't echo her expression. If she couldn't understand how important this next week was for me, there wasn't anything I could do to explain it to her. I had hoped she would be there to support me. If she insisted on acting like a child, maybe it would be better if I sent her away.

"No catch. I want you to have a nice birthday. You can take my jet and stay at my house in Beverly Hills." I didn't offer it like a trap, but part of me hoped she would refuse and insist on staying here to support me.

Her chin inclined and her pouty lip receded. "Well, how about I stay for the dinner and leave the day after that?"

So much for support.

It seemed like a reasonable enough compromise, but something about it still stung. I tried to make the fact we would spend her birthday on separate coasts less awkward. "Maybe if everything goes well and I get done soon, I can join you early next week?"

"Yeah," she said a little too casual. The way she pulled her shoulders back and took a few steps nearer, closing the gap between us, showed she was happy now.

"So, did you want to run out for coffee?" I offered, willing to put her birthday weekend aside to spend some time with her now.

"Nah, I'm going to try to get in for a hair appointment since I'll be leaving Saturday. It's short notice." Her eyes washed over my desk, and she added, "You said this is a crazy week for you, so I might as well let you work." When she replanted her gaze on me, her voice sounded happy. "But I'll see you tomorrow for dinner, right?"

"Of course." I held her gaze, wanting to tell her how much I hated this.

Hated the distance growing between us.

Hated the avoidance of certain topics.

Hated the way we were fighting.

But as much as I wanted to tell her that, she seemed so distracted. As if to prove my point, she pulled out her phone. Probably already texting her friends back in LA. I wasn't jealous. I was happy I could be the one to put the smile back on her face, but even then, I could feel things changing. The distance between us felt like a gaping hole.

"All right, see you later." She leaned over on one foot and planted a chaste kiss on my lips. Before I could say another word, she headed out the door, her eyes on her phone the whole way.

Once she was gone, my eyes pulled to my desk. My brain told me I needed to get to work, but my heart felt heavy. The front door slammed, announcing Tonya had officially let herself out. Even though we parted on supposedly "good" terms, something felt symbolic about that door slam. It wasn't a finality but another layer in this weird limbo we'd been in. This was a gray area, and I didn't like gray.

I was the type of person who was a black-and-white thinker.

I knew something or I didn't.

I liked something or I didn't. There was no wishy-washy back-and-forth with me.

I'd loved Tonya at one time, but now I don't.

That didn't make me a jerk.

I didn't want to fall out of love with her, but she wasn't the person I had loved anymore.

But I couldn't *tell* her that.

That would take communication skills.

My communication skills were deficient.

I headed to the attic.

Four

Atalie

Back at home that night, I was on a mission to come up with the perfect smoothie recipe. Not that I was a huge smoothie connoisseur, but I had a pile of past-due produce that no one should ever really eat. I had made friends with the man at the fruit and vegetable stand. He was going to toss this spread into the trash before I begged him to give it to me.

I clearly was out of pride.

With my random waves of low blood sugar this morning, my skipping breakfast had proved to be something which had snuck up on me in a bad way, nearly making me sick. I was hoping smoothies would be something slick in the morning I could drink to settle my sensitive stomach.

With a spoon, I scraped a little off the top of my blended concoction and held it out for Josiah to taste. "Try this one." His cerulean eyes—which melted my heart more than any other pair on the planet—popped wide and he sealed his lips. "Come on, Bud." I moved the spoon a little closer to his lips while cupping my free hand underneath the spoon just like I used to do when he was a toddler.

"Mom, it's puke green."

"That's because I added a little spinach, but you can't taste it and it'll give you energy."

"Yes, yes, you can taste it." He sealed his lips back up and gave me his I-can-totally-out-last-you-in-stubbornness glare.

"Don't waste it." Disappointed he wasn't totally on board with my new food plan, I moved the spoon to my mouth. "Look, I'm going to try it." The moment the mush hit my taste buds, my tongue lurched forward in reflex, trying to push the horrid blend out.

"See!" Josiah pointed to my pinched lips. "I told you it's gross. You're going to puke." He was right! Covering my mouth, I fled to the sink, letting it spill out. I shuddered as the last of the chunks dripped off my chin. It wasn't so much the taste, but the regurgitated, chewed-cud texture had made it impossible to pallet.

Josiah came in next to me, handing me a dish towel. "See. You puked."

"I did not." I reached back and snatched the towel, taking a moment to dab my chin. "It was sabotage because you made me laugh." I could tell by his stare he wasn't buying it, and I knew I was never making *that* recipe again.

"I can't believe you ate that."

Running my tongue over the front of my teeth, I willed my mind not to taste the remnants. "I don't think I swallowed any of it. It was more a lingering on my tongue." My admittance sent Josiah into a fit of laughter. "Okay." I dumped the cud into the garbage disposal and replaced the rinsed-out pitcher on the base. "Time for a new recipe. What do you think? Should we try more citrus next time?"

His lips pulled into a sly smile that revealed his two missing teeth. Not the front teeth because that would have been Christmas-card adorable, but the two next to those. They'd been missing for months, and I was beginning to wonder if the adult teeth would ever grow in. He dramatically winced. "What's this *we* stuff?"

"We have to leave early. I need something I can prep the night before." I hiked a warning brow at him before I emptied more ice into the pitcher. "Just because my first attempt was a failure, doesn't mean I'm giving up."

His eyes widened dubiously as he scanned my spread of veggies that were laid out on the counter. "In that case, I agree you need to add way more citrus." He dramatically snatched two oranges and started to roll them on the counter, prepping them for peeling. "I'll pick my own recipe."

It took another dozen or so batches before I found the right combo, but once I did, I knew it was the golden nugget: mango, strawberry, blueberry, and lime for raw ingredients. Then I added powdered greens—they were less cud textured than the raw ones—for digestion, coconut oil to make it slick on the swallow, and acai powder for an immunity boost. In my shaker only, I also added in my secret weight management blend, and it was better than a five o'clock cocktail.

Well, maybe I wouldn't go that far, but it was edible.

After another sleepless night, I was up early again—not like a regular early morning that most people went to work. Early as a crazy and obsessive person stuck in nocturnal mode. I dug through my headbands and tried to find the perfect one that made my new hair layers look intentional. Once I added loose curls, it didn't look too bad.

Okay, the phrase "blow-dried-poodle head" came to mind, but I was out of options until I got paid and could afford a real haircut.

Now that I was ready, all I had left to do was deal with this impending feeling of doom budding in my chest. As much as I tried to force positive thoughts, I didn't want to go back to that house. It had been humiliating meeting my boss like that. I'm not sure how it hadn't been enough embarrassment to kill me. In an odd way it didn't surprise me, though. Just another notch on the this-year-can't-get-any-worse belt I was forced to wear.

I really had no idea what I was even doing anymore.

The one thing I did know . . .

I was doing everything I could for Josiah. I never planned on raising him alone. We were in a new city, starting over with no help. It was all so overwhelming, but he had no one else but me. With that as my sole motivation—it was still excruciating—I fought back tears and laced up my Alice sneakers.

The noisy bathroom pipe sounded from across the hall, confirming Josiah was awake with his scrolling thoughts again. It was way too early to go to work, but in a way, I was happy because we'd have time to walk to the beach again. That walk was the reason I had applied for the job in the first place, because I didn't have a car. I had originally wanted a nanny job. I figured watching a child similar to Josiah's age would make it easy to bring him along. None of that mattered because no references meant no interviews. When I saw the ad for my position and noticed it was within walking distance, I took it as a sign. It really was my only option which made my terrible first day so much more suffocating.

This morning when we arrived at the house, I heard ear-screeching clanking noises. Tracing the sound to the kitchen, I found Mrs. Michael yanking out a pan, then she rejected it, tossing it noisily back into the cupboard. "You'd think he'd have a nine by thirteen in here somewhere."

Squinting, like closing my eyes would help to block the cacophony, I set my smoothie shaker on the counter. "It doesn't look like he does much cooking." I kept one eye on Josiah as he plopped down at the table and busied himself with setting out his schoolbooks. When satisfied he didn't need my help, I arched a brow back at her. "What are you trying to make?"

"A birthday cake," she said in a huff.

"Is it Trey's birthday?"

"No, it's Tonya's." She banged around in the cabinet again.

"And who is Tonya?"

"That's his girlfriend and he's throwing her a party."

"Oh, that makes sense." I gave up waiting for her to wake the dead and walked to the little cupboard next to the fridge. I had cleaned it out yesterday, arranging everything into a single stack of stainless-steel pans, all stowed according to size. I was easily able to grab the exact one she needed. "Here." I set it on the counter in front of her, letting out a breath of relief because she could finally be quiet. "This looks like it is a nine by thirteen."

"Oh, thank you." Her eyes flicked back to the cupboard. "I was going to try that one next." She took the pan and slid it across the counter to where she had set up a baking station with mostly normal-looking baking ingredients. I raised a brow when I landed on a stray can of tomato soup and a brand-new jar of mayonnaise.

"So, when does the party start?" I asked as I went to the broom closet and grabbed my broom and dustpan.

"I don't know for sure." Her eyes steadied forward as she read her recipe. In a monotone voice, she added, "You know how it is with family."

My chin inclined to a curious position, but I stayed quiet, vowing to mind my business.

"She's plastic." Her comment seemed to float in the air like it didn't even come from her.

"Pardon me?"

"Tonya, she has more plastic parts than a cheap lawn mower." She shook her head, like she was feeling shame. "I wouldn't want to sit next to her in a hot tub. You'd find floaties."

The immature child in my brain wanted to chuckle. Yet, I managed to bite it back. "It can't be that bad."

"I've known her since she was fifteen when Trey took her to the Snowball Dance. She used to be such a natural beauty. Ever since she moved to California, she's always remodeling something." Her eyes shifted, landing on my smoothie shaker. "Isn't it a little early to be drinking?"

"It's not that kind of a drink." I shot her a sassy grin. "It's my famous smoothie recipe. Well, famous as of last night." I picked up the shaker and opened the lid so she could see the royal blue color. "I wanted something healthy. Plus, it's an easy way for me to slip in my secret weight control supplements." I held it closer to her face and urged, "Smell it."

Taking the bait, she leaned her nose forward. "That doesn't smell too bad, but how does it taste?"

"It tastes good. Even Josiah liked this one." I set the shaker back on the counter and offered, "I can make you one and bring it over tomorrow if you want to try it?"

I thought for sure she'd sneer at the idea, but instead, she gave me a sideways glance. "Sure . . . I can try one."

"All right, I'll bring you one." I felt proud she was willing to try my famous, to me and Josiah, smoothie.

Then she looked back at her baking project like she noticed it for the first time. "Oh, I better get to work here. I want it to have time to cool so I can frost it before the party."

"Right," I agreed, hoping she wasn't going to use the mayonnaise as frosting on a tomato-flavored cake. I sighed to myself, releasing a hint of a giggle. I gripped my broom loosely, sweeping in the opposite direction, away from her, and called back, "Well, enjoy the party."

With an extra smoothie shaker tucked in the nook of my arm, Josiah and I moved like mice as we made our way to the kitchen the following morning. Mrs. Michael sat at the table with a porcelain mug of coffee, still piping out of the top. I was beginning to wonder if she had a house of her own, even though she insisted she did.

"Good morning," I said in my best cheery voice, trying hard to want to be here today. "You're at 'em early this morning."

Her lips curled into a pleasant-enough smile. "I'm a morning person."

"I brought your smoothie." I held up the shaker before I slid it in front of her. "Try it."

She opened the flip lid, taking a small sip. Then she lowered it, leveling it with her eyes as she studied the outside. "That's good. Not at all what I was expecting."

Josiah cut in with an amused voice, "You're lucky you didn't get the prototypes."

Her eyes that matched Trey's locked on him, and her pale lips bent up at the corner. "Were they that bad?"

Josiah pretended to dry heave. "It was like eating garbage."

Mrs. Michael pointed to the shaker in her hand. "But you'll drink this one?"

"That one is acceptable."

"Well, if this helps control my weight, I'll be your biggest fan." She started to take another sip, but her action was thwarted when the front door flew open and shut. I turned, expecting to see Trey, but instead, it was a tall ginger-haired woman who had curves that would make a Southern back road jealous.

"Well, good morning, Tonya," Mrs. Michael called from her place at the table. "It's early for you to be here."

Tonya's gaze held forward. "I'd have to say the same thing to you." When her breath blew out, it brought the smell of meatloaf with it and not like a soul-food, cooking from the South meatloaf. More like *a soggy, left in the fridge for days, but I gotta choke it down to avoid being wasteful* scent. It made me wonder how a woman so pretty could overlook a detail that foul-smelling. My stomach hurled at her meat-infused breath as I watched her blow right past us, down the hall.

"He's still upstairs in his room," Mrs. Michael called after her, but the only sound we heard was footsteps ascending the stairs.

"She seems like a lovely woman," I said, a little dismayed.

"She's not really," Mrs. Michael said into the open lid of her shaker before taking another generous drink.

I struggled to hold back a snort, and thankfully, somehow managed to leave that comment alone by acting distracted as I checked the time on my watch. I moved toward the steps before calling back, "Enjoy your smoothie. I need to get started upstairs today. Your son had said something about making sure the entertainment room was cleaned because he's having company tonight."

"Oh, yes." Her voice sounded like it was inviting gossip. "It's investor suck-up week."

"Really?" Looking back at her, I waited in case she wanted to expand, but she didn't. That was okay, because her comment had put me in a melancholy mood, reminding me of my own husband, who had also been a businessman—well, an accidental one.

My husband had lived with the soul of an artist and all he ever wanted to do was create. For him to bring his art to his customers, he had bought an old brick building right on the main drag of our small town. It drained every penny we had ever saved, and even then, some more. Without even one buck left over for renovations, we taught ourselves every handyman skill we needed to remodel it into a studio.

The art studio paid for itself, but not any extra, so to pay our bills, he had bought the building next to it to put in a gift shop. The following year, the building on the other side of the studio went into a foreclosure auction. We eagerly acquired that building to expand into a large events venue. None of his businesses ever became overly lucrative, and we always had to stretch to take on more debt. I remembered clearly how stressful those investor meetings had been. Now the stress which had clouded those moments had been lifted and I saw those memories through a gilded filter. *I'd give anything to go back.*

A storm of footsteps unleashed, barreling down the stairs. Tonya flew around the corner, and I thought she would ignore us again, but instead, she stopped, squaring her body with Mrs. Michael, who was still at the table. Trey was right on her heel and first to speak. "Tonya, let me handle this."

Tonya parked her hand on her hip and gave Mrs. Michael *a please go check yourself into the nursing home* glare. "Are you finally going to tell your mom to butt out?"

Mrs. Michael sucked in a loud gasp, her eyes flying to her son.

Trey immediately cut in, "No, I'm not going to say that."

"Trey," Tonya seemed to be almost pleading with him. "She got me a T-shirt that said, 'Nobody's Home.' She was basically telling me I'm dumb."

His chest rose slowly, and his eyes locked on his mother. "Tonya and I were talking, and she's a little hurt by the gifts you gave her last night." His eyes bounced back to his girlfriend for a moment before bringing them back to his mom. "I can understand why. I know you didn't mean to offend her, but maybe in the future you can stick to gift cards?"

Mrs. Michael triple blinked while she looked back at her son. "I don't understand how you can be mad at me for getting her presents."

He moved closer to his mom, reaching an arm around her shoulder. "We can talk more about it later, but right now everyone needs to calm down." His stressed eyes landed back on Tonya. "Right?"

"Not right." Tonya stuck her jaw forward. "I want an apology."

Trey buried his free hand deep into the front of his dark hair, letting it slide down the back of his head, before hooking it on his neck. "I know you do, but I don't think she is going to see it your way. It's best to give us all some time to think and let me talk to her later."

Mrs. Michael's head turned to stare at her son. "Talk to me about what?"

Nodding his head like it would help him get his words out, he said, "This whole thing. We need to talk, but I can't do it now. I have prep to do. So"—he spread his arms out in front of him and pushed them to the sides, like he was wiping a desk clean— "can we let this go for now and I'll come back to it next week?"

"Sure." Mrs. Michael shrugged with her face. "I don't see what there is to let go, but that's fine." She picked up her shaker, but Tonya was steadfast on giving her a *I'll check you into the nursing home myself* glare. After a moment of hot silence, Mrs. Michael's brow bent down, and she held her shaker out, offering it to Tonya. "You know, you really need to try this weight loss shake."

The noise that escaped from Tonya's sealed lips sounded like a wild animal. Her fake-baked hands flew up in rage and she shrieked, "See what I mean? I can't do this anymore!" Then she spun on her heel without another word, darting out the door.

"She wasn't calling you fat!" Trey beckoned after her, but it was too late because the door slammed shut, silencing us all.

Perfectly on cue, Mrs. Michael bucked a brow at her son. "How rude was that?"

Five

Atalie

It was late in the afternoon, and I was exhausted by the time I had finished getting the house cleaned. Josiah was flashing me a *get me out of here* expression and I hurried to get my supplies put away and offered, "Should we grab some food on the way home and eat it in the park by the beach?"

That put a smile on his lips. "Cheeseburgers from Jerry's?"

"Deal." His eyes locked on mine, and my heart swelled from how easy it was to please him. On top of that joy, the better news was it was payday! I was so ready to treat us both to a celebratory meal and get back to having a more normal life. Unfortunately, as I was tying up my trash bag, the front door opened again.

Trey, his mother, and Tonya all walked inside. Their faces were sober but not upset like this morning. Trey's phone beeped and he immediately buried his attention into his palm, so engrossed he didn't even notice he had walked past his office door when he groaned, "You have got to be kidding me."

"What happened?" Tonya walked up beside him, trying to steal a peek at his phone.

"The caterers I hired for tonight's dinner meeting had to cancel. It seems lame, but I need things to go smoothly so I can focus on talking to Jane and Allen."

"Could you call a temp agency?" Tonya asked.

"The party starts in two hours. I don't see that happening." He let one hand roll over his forehead when he added, "We'll have to order food from a restaurant and set it up self-serve."

I don't know why, but this reminded of the time when I had gone with my husband to dinner with the guy who he had bought his studio from. The guy had wanted a cash offer and we didn't even have a pot to put a penny in—let alone buy a building for cash—but my husband had insisted we try to win him over. He offered to take the owner out for drinks and the guy drank top-shelf whiskey all night, which put us over our modest credit card limit. Of course, our card declined when we tried to pay, but we couldn't let the guy know we couldn't buy the drinks because we were trying to get him to agree to sell us his building. While they were closing their deal, I excused myself to the bathroom, snuck back and found the owner, and begged him to let me wash dishes for a month on the condition he didn't utter even a tiny word about our bill. It worked; the owner agreed. I got some rock-toned arms from lifting those heavy trays of bar glasses all month. In addition, we were able to get our guy to agree to sell us the property. Pulling my eyes to the side, I blinked back a reminiscent gaze just as I heard Mrs. Michael speak up, "Trey, maybe Atalie can stay for a little while to help out?"

Trey's eyes fell on me, and he made a face, looking surprised to see me there before checking his watch. "Isn't it late for you to even be here?"

I gave a curt nod, trying to act chill and not like the nerd who hyper-obsessed about the cleanliness of his house in an effort to make up for drowning his computer my first day. In my best casual tone, I tossed out, "I wanted to make sure everything was ready for you tonight." Then I motioned to Josiah, who impatiently sat in the kitchen with his book bag on his back like he was a caged racehorse waiting for the gate to open. "We were on our way out to grab dinner, but I guess . . . if you *need* me to stay, I can stay."

Trey's eyes drifted to Josiah, pausing a little longer than what would have been expected, before I realized I hadn't ever introduced them. "That's my son, Josiah. He's been coming with me." I had anticipated Trey to smile and greet him like most people who saw how adorable he was—mom bias. Instead, his face stayed straight, making me apprehensive, so I added, "I guess, your mom said it was fine." I continued to eye his side profile, waiting for an upward twitch of a lip, a wave or heck, anything to indicate he was done staring at my son, but he stayed fixated on Josiah. As the seconds ticked on, it grew odder because he wasn't trying to engage him at all. He was just silently watching him. "Is . . . that okay?" I finally asked.

His blinks interrupted his eye lock, and he replanted his focus on me and rushed to say, "Ah, I appreciate your help getting everything cleaned, but I can try some numbers. It's only been a few days without a paper shredder attack. I'm sure you're probably still needing to recoup."

Mrs. Michael stood up from her chair, cutting off her son, "Trey, I think you should accept her offer because you might not find anyone else on short notice, and you know how Jane gets. She's a handful."

Before Trey could respond, Tonya's face took a look of worry as she spoke to Trey like I wasn't in the room. "I don't think that will work for her to stay for the party. What's she supposed to wear?" Her hand whisked toward me. "She's a filthy mess."

For the first time in my life, I had the urge to growl like an angry dog. Sure, I wasn't wearing makeup, and my painting smock wasn't couture fashion, but I was fully hygienic! I could never pass for the filthy mess category.

Before I was forced to make an awkward reply, Mrs. Michael came to my rescue with a remark directed at Tonya, "Maybe, since you're leaving early, you can grab her one of those fancy dresses your stylist sends you and you can have a driver bring it back." There was a sisterhood moment we shared when her eyes landed on mine. I was grateful she was stepping up until she added in a thoughtful voice, "Oh wait, that's not going to work. She can't wear one of your dresses. It'll be *huge* on her."

Tonya had a *screw the nursing home, I'll lock you in the basement* glare directed at Mrs. Michael when she muttered, "See what I mean, Trey?"

Waving his hands in front of him like he was desperate to clear the air of smothering exhaust, he said, "I'm not doing this."

The corners of Mrs. Michael's mouth drooped. "What did I do now?"

Tonya snapped back at her, "You insulted my body size."

"I wasn't insulting you." Mrs. Michael motioned to her. "I was simply pointing out the obvious. She is much thinner than you are."

Trey wrapped his arm around his mother, his shoulders bounced like he was suppressing an inward chuckle that pained him. "Mom, please, it's sort of that thing we talked about where sometimes your opinion is needed and we will ask you and appreciate it, but right now is not that time."

Her eyes bounced back to Tonya, but she sucked in her bottom lip and held her feet steady in her place. "Well, can you have your stylist select something for Atalie in her size?"

"No, she doesn't work weekends." Tonya's face was still a shade of red when she looked back at me again, and wearily offered, "I can send one of mine along. I'll throw a belt in with it, and you can at least try it."

"Sure," I quickly agreed, knowing the clock was ticking.

"Great." She glanced back at Trey briefly, before walking toward the door, adding, "I'll run home now."

I reluctantly turned to Trey to confirm, "So you do need us to stay to help you tonight?"

His head tilted like he was having the largest headache of his life. With his eyes locked on Tonya while she walked out the door, he commented, "If you think you can handle it."

"We'll be fine." I turned my head to Josiah, feeling mom guilt wash over me. "Right? You're used to boring old-people parties from your dad?"

"I'll be fine." His words gravitated down into a mutter at the end. When his eyes hit mine, I predicted the negotiation he was going to throw my way. "As long as we can still order Jerry's?"

I winked at him, feeling grateful he was so easy to please. "Deal."

Trey fixed his eyes back on me. "Thank you. I know it's last-minute, but I appreciate it." Then he tucked his hands in his pockets and headed upstairs.

"Well, I guess that's my cue to go get my hair done," Mrs. Michael announced. "You kids have fun tonight and I'll see you in the morning." Relief washed over me, knowing she wasn't planning to attend tonight's party. Even though I had grown oddly fond of her because she made things entertaining, I knew the evening would go much smoother without her, so I smiled and waved goodbye.

Six

Trey

Meeting Josiah was like having a weird out-of-body flashback to my childhood. I shuddered, remembering how my mom had cleaned houses too to make ends meet the first year after my dad had died. I distinctly remembered sitting at her boss's table, waiting for her to get off work on so many nights. *That kid*—wearing a pretty sweet *Star Wars* T-shirt—looked like he could have been me. I pushed the memory away and headed upstairs. It wasn't at all what I needed to be thinking about right now. But everything else that had happened today wasn't much better. I hated everything about today.

I hated Tonya leaving to go to California.

I hated my mom being weird toward Tonya.

I hated that I had to have this stupid meeting tonight.

But most of all, I hated that I had to have this meeting without my business partner, who helped me start this company. Because I knew if he'd been here . . . it wouldn't be failing.

Damion had been the smooth talker, the extrovert who had helped me get my first date with Tonya when we were only fifteen. Without me knowing it, he'd called her pretending to be me. This was before cell phones and caller ID—the good old days when we could do the coolest pranks with a phone when we were bored. He knew I liked her and talked to her for days, prepping her full of all my less-annoying qualities until finally asking her out to the Snowball Dance for me, which was where we did the switcharoo and I showed up.

That wasn't the end of his victories. He talked a cop out of giving me a speeding ticket when I was sixteen. I still didn't know how he managed that one because I was going ninety and I rightfully should have had my hearing adjusted for that recklessness. However, his most amazing achievement was convincing my mom to agree to send me to coding camp when I was in middle school. It sounded like a normal thing, but she had to use her last four hundred dollars to afford it. Lucky for us both, that one paid off. I wasn't good with people, but I could lose myself in code for days, feeling like that was exactly how my brain was wired to be.

We started a company together. Well, I did all the work, and once a year Damion would fly out and do my schmoozing. If there is one thing I understood about business, it was that every business needed a smooth talker. Since Damion wasn't here anymore, I was floundering, wishing he'd at least left me some footnotes. I flashed my eyes heavenward and whispered, "You'd better help me, man."

Checking my watch, I noted that I didn't have much time, but thanks to Atalie the house didn't smell ancient anymore, so I did what I always did when I needed to clear my head and headed to the attic.

My place of solace and meditation.

My place of reflection and healing.

My place of escapism and remembrance that gave me strength to face my future.

I always had to give the little door more than a gentle nudge to get it to open, and once it became unstuck, the hinges would wail in welcome. I should do some maintenance on them so they'd be quieter, and it was silly, but I had an attachment to the sound because they had always done that, even since before my dad passed.

My dad had been a ship captain.

One of the best ship captains—or at least he was in my eyes.

He was always gone for weeks and sometimes months, and I'd await his return anxiously. He'd usually get back late after I'd gone to bed, but like a signal from a secret club, I heard that creak while I lay in bed, and my heart would swell because it meant my dad was trekking up to the attic.

The sound meant he was *home.*

In his life, this had been my dad's den—a man cave. No staff was allowed in there, and even my mom stayed away. Only I was allowed inside. I'd climb on his knee, and he always had a story for me from his most recent adventures. He'd empty his pockets and drop several shiny foreign coins onto the rustic surface of the wood table.

They were a treasure to me.

I'd scoop them up, studying each one before stowing them safely into a wooden chest he had given me. He never treated me like an interruption and when the stories ran out, we'd do "man things" like build ship models together or play Chess. Even though it abruptly ended, those moments—stolen from the night—grounded me more than anything else I had lived through.

I yanked on the shoestring cord which illuminated the single light bulb, letting my eyes wander along the wood panel walls, taking in each memory. My favorite: a model of an American Schooner that we had built together. Okay, he did most of it while I sat on his lap and drank root beer, but it felt like a group effort.

Behind that hung an old, tattered map—one he had used in his youth before modern technology. A trail of red ink outlined the routes he had taken connecting the port on Long Island all the way to Canada, England, Panama and through the canal. I let my fingers trace each route as I had done since I was a boy, and then around Cape Horn, where I always stopped. A single point, traceable on any map and where the Atlantic meets the Pacific and where he was last seen, or as I chose to reference it as—*where he rests.*

Staring at that spot of my dad's finality on the map always did everything to help put things into proper perspective for me. There wasn't much I felt I couldn't face when I thought about what my dad went through. Even a stupid investor meeting—as nauseous as that made me—was trivial compared to that.

Seven

Atalie

I hated to admit it, but Mrs. Michael had been right about the dress being huge on me. It looked like a giant sloppy sack of potatoes. I used the belt Tonya had sent along, cinching it tight.

Now I was a potato sack with a belt.

I don't think I ever felt less elegant, but I lifted my chin and set off. My job was to wear this sack of potatoes and conquer this dinner party.

The doorbell rang, and I thought it was the guests, but instead, I met Trey at the door as he received his food order in eight large bags. "Wow, that's a lot of food." I eyed the row of sacks he had made by the door. "What did you order?"

"Jane likes seafood, so I went with a shrimp and rice thing."

Grabbing two bags, I carried them to the side buffet in the dining room to unpack them and found two large containers of rice from each bag. "I found the rice," I said and dumped two of the containers into a holding dish. Then I replaced the other rice containers in a sack to move them to the kitchen oven to hold them as extra. I opened the next bag and found two more containers of rice. I closed those back up and set them aside as well and called over to Trey, who was bringing me the rest of the bags. "Boy, you ordered a lot of rice. Do you have the bag with the shrimp?"

Peeking in one sack, he reported, "Uh, this one is more rice." His brow lowered, as he opened another sack which thankfully had a different shaped container and he pulled it out to find one breadstick.

"I don't get it," I said, as one was such an odd number.

"I'm pretty sure when I made the order it was for one basket of bread. They must have thought I wanted just one."

"Okay, well, we shouldn't set that out because there isn't enough for everyone." I raised my chin, trying to see in the next bag. "What else do you have?"

He opened the last sack and as soon as his eyes hit the bottom, he let out a confused chuckle and pulled out a small bowl with a clear lid, displaying six small shrimp. "I ordered six," Trey explained. "I meant meals, but it looks like they gave me only six shrimp instead." Before either of us could answer, the doorbell rang, and Trey's eyes grew large. "They are here, and we have nothing to serve."

Already knowing we had no other food in the house because I had just cleaned out the fridge, I stared back. "What do you want me to do?"

He pulled out his wallet, slid his credit card out, and handed it to me. "You order a pizza and I'll stall."

I took his card, then added in a thoughtful voice, "I'll invent some sort of appetizer with what we have, and you can serve drinks until the pizza arrives."

He took a longer than average pause while he looked at me and offered a heartfelt, "Thank you." Lowering my eyes, I smiled sweetly and said, "No problem." I hurriedly grabbed the bags of rice, moving them to the kitchen where I recruited Josiah to help me fashion creative-looking plates of breadstick bites.

"Good thing rich people are used to small portions," I said as I picked up my tray en route to the dining room.

As soon as we were through the door, I heard, "He is a handsome young man." My eyes followed the voice, landing on one of the women at the table. It didn't take a genius to see this woman was wealthy—or at least she wanted people to think she was—with layers of heavy gold chains around her neck, and diamonds on almost every finger.

I lowered my tray, taking one plate off, placing it in front of her. "He's my amazing helper." I smiled politely, then I looked across the table at Trey. He had this nervous grin on his face, highlighted with a flustered glow on his cheekbones. Even though this was his party, he looked oddly out of place sitting in the middle of two couples and he appeared to be doing most of the listening. It was cringey to watch as I served the rest of my appetizers, and I was glad to be able to disappear back into the kitchen.

I had assumed the conversation would warm up to laughter and smiles, but when I came back out to serve the pizza, it seemed to be even more awkward with both couples carrying on their own separate conversations. "Can I get you anything else?" I waited for instructions.

"No, thank you," Trey said. I started to leave, but he got up and followed me back into the kitchen. When we were out of their earshot, he planted his eyes on mine and the worry I had seen earlier in the dinner had obviously leveled up. "I don't think anyone wants to eat. They prefer drinks and keep looking at their watches."

Perfectly on cue, the woman—who I had spoken with earlier—appeared in the kitchen door, leaning in like she didn't dare take a step farther inside. "I'm sorry to interrupt but can you grab my coat?"

Trey went stone-faced, his eyes sending out warning signs of alert. I waited for him to take control of the conversation and convince her to stay—or shoot, say something—but he just stood there gawking. It floored me how a businessman could be so inept when it came to working a crowd. So, I sprang forward, placing a soft touch on her forearm, and in a disappointed voice, asked, "Already? You haven't had a chance to see the art collection upstairs." I made up words as I spoke, but it sounded good once they were out, so I went along with it. Her eyes locked on the front door, a little too longingly, but I urged, "You won't regret it."

She relented with a shrug. "Maybe a little while longer."

"Good." I slid my lips eagerly into a grin. "Give me one second and I'll come back out to give you the tour."

She took one more look of acknowledgment at Trey before bowing out of the kitchen.

Both Trey and I let out a synchronized sigh, but even after his deep release, his breathing was loud and measured. "That's Jane." His voice was low and concealed. "She's my worst nightmare."

"I can tell." I bit back a grin, feeling like I had entered some crazy nut house. "I'll do my best to keep her busy, but don't waste any time. I don't know how long I can entertain her." Tugging on the already straight collar of his shirt, like it would give him confidence, he shot me a look of exasperation before heading back to the table.

I reluctantly met Jane on the bottom of the stairs, pretending to be cheerful. Thankfully, I had hosted tons of art exhibits and I was able to say something thought-provoking about each piece. I didn't recognize the first painting, but I could tell by the depths of the paint strokes and the patina it was an original of a large cargo ship. It wasn't the nautical theme of the painting that made the hair on my arms stand up, but something about the artist's style. It seemed so familiar but after double-checking the back and still not finding a signature, I had nothing to go on as far as its origin. I gave up trying to guess and moved on to the next one. The next one stumped me just as much as it was another ship, same artist and no signature. "It is so unusual to see an original painting of this quality not have a signature," I commented.

"Right. If I could paint like that, I would have my name in giant letters all over the bottom."

"Me too."

"I'm impressed with your knowledge." Jane gave me a suspicious side-eye like she still wasn't sure if I should be allowed in some secret club of hers.

"My previous life gave me a lot of time in an art studio, entertaining people."

Without another word, she leaned back against the wall, taking her sweet time studying the piece. The fact she continued to ignore the business negotiations downstairs—that were meant to include her—gave her a strong air of arrogance, like she didn't value people's time.

It was another hour before Jane asked for her coat again. I walked her downstairs, with a strained smile on my lips. When I shot Trey a warning look, he gave me a permissive nod, signaling it would be okay. As soon as the front door was shut behind their backs, he blurted out, "I'm so glad that's over. I'm sweating so bad; my back is drenched." He dramatically untucked his shirt, and I could literally see the streaks of a sweat stain through his white shirt. "I have never been so nervous in my life." He took another big breath. "John and his wife declined right away. I had expected that. Allen wasn't giving me much feedback but when his wife was ready to leave, I knew if he would have left with her, it would have been over."

I spoke in a low voice. "So, is everything good?"

"No, not good, but it's better." His tone was even, but unconvincing. I didn't offer any further comment because it wasn't my place to pry. Instead, he broke the pause first. "Let's go grab Josiah and I'll give you guys a ride home since it's so late."

I pushed my bottom lip out in reflex and immediately rebutted, "No, it's fine. We can walk." We didn't live far, but I didn't dare tell him I was practically in his neighborhood.

His look said he wasn't hearing it. "No, it's not okay. It's way too late for you two to be walking alone."

I waved my hand in a dismissing way. I did *not* want him to see where we lived! I wasn't ashamed of it. It was the opposite. Thanks to my departed mother-in-law, the house we lived in was exceptionally nice—not as nice as his. Nevertheless, it was prime real estate near the beach, and it would be impossible without telling him all the details of my private life to explain to him why I had to clean his house while living in a beach house. "I can call a ride share."

"There's no need." He assured me and headed back through the house. "I was so nervous, I didn't have a drop to drink, and the fresh air would do me some good."

I raced to find Josiah to get him out the door before Trey further insisted. At first, my eyes grew in alarm because I couldn't see him anywhere. Then Trey pointed to the high-back armchair in the corner, where Josiah had slouched way down; his eyelids hooded, fast asleep. My lips pulled up in the corners at the sight of how adorable—mom biased—he was and picked up a glass from the table. "Well, if he's sleeping, I might as well finish cleaning up."

Trey interrupted my actions by firmly stating, "You are not doing that now."

I ignored him and pushed the chairs back neatly at the table. "The more I do now, the less I have to do in the morning."

He followed me as I continued to gather more glasses. "No, I insist."

"I'm only going to take care of the stuff that would attract bugs." Collecting another glass, I was about to cross the room to grab the last stray glass on the buffet, but he cut in front, blocking me.

"If you don't leave that alone, I'm going to get my paper shredder." His lips slid easily over his perfect teeth, pinning an amused smile on his face.

"Shreddergate 2.0," I easily made fun of myself.

His lips held on to his smile, but his face took a more stoic expression when he appeared to change the subject, "I might actually owe you an apology."

"An apology for what?"

"I might have misjudged you. You were a huge help tonight. I'm sorry if I haven't been acting like I appreciated your help, but it turned out you are much better with people than you are with shredders."

A laugh escaped from my lips at the same time I looked up to meet his gaze. His eyes clung to mine, and a crazy magnetic pull seemed to trap me. In all honesty, he looked weary, but beneath that was something else which made the heat in my cheeks turn on. He was handsome, I knew that. However, his gaze penetrated so deep, it made the breath in my chest shallow.

Neither one of us flinched. Like a schoolgirl in an awkward first encounter, my feet stayed cemented to the floor. I let my bottom lip curl up under my top row of teeth, but still my eyes steadied with his. Finally, when I was about to give up, thinking we'd be frozen like that forever, he broke the trance by saying, "Will you stop working and go home?" He winced, and immediately backed on the heels of his words, catching me in another eye trap, like he was checking to make sure he somehow didn't offend me. I wasn't insulted but I didn't have it in me for another face-burning stare, so I looked away.

I turned my head back to Josiah, who was piping out the quietest of snores from his cute little button nose. Trey moved forward and without waiting for a rebuttal, he scooped him up, saying, "How about I load him into one of my cars? You can drive it home and bring it back in the morning."

My breath lightened, knowing I was being released from having to make up a bad excuse. "Yeah, that'll be perfect."

He continued in a hushed voice, "Actually, why don't you take a few extra days off? I'll be leaving to visit Tonya, and I won't be here."

He didn't have to tell me twice, and we didn't talk anymore as he led me to the oversized garage where several nice cars were waiting. He helped us into the closest one, and I didn't ask what make or model the car was, because I didn't want to be nervous driving it. I simply drove off, feeling glad I had helped Trey because even though it had been awkward, it was obvious the guy needed help.

EIGHT

Atalie

After a few days off, I led Josiah out the door with two extra smoothies in my hand. We were down about a block before Josiah brought up something we hadn't spoken about in weeks. "Mom, how much longer is it going to be before we can go home?"

My voice caught in my airway because although that had been my original goal when we came here—to work our way to being able to return home—I wasn't sure if I could go back. Aside from all the financial stuff that was a huge mess, I still didn't need to see all the sorry-your-life-sucks faces. I answered as truthfully as I could, "I don't know. Your dad wasn't planning all of this, so his stuff wasn't set up right. I thought for sure we'd have things worked out by now, but the longer it's been, the more I learn, and he had owed some people some money and some of that stuff is hard to fix." I looked over at him. "It's grown-up stuff, though, and you don't need to worry about it."

"I know, but I miss my friends." His voice was sort of listless, making my heart ache.

"I'm sure you do." I made sure to keep my voice even to not apply pressure on him. "Do you think you want to try to go back to regular school to be with kids your own age?" His lips pursed out like a duck. The longer he held them like that, the more I considered maybe he was ready to go back. Maybe he hadn't told me already because he was trying to be strong for me. With a lowered voice, I added, "Josiah, you can tell me if you want to return. I understand."

"I don't really mind online school," he said after a long minute, "but it would be nice to meet some friends here."

"Well . . ." I looked forward as we walked, as this conversation was so out of the blue and I hadn't been prepared for it. "There're only a few weeks left in the regular school year, so maybe you finish out what you have and then we enroll in the spring for a fresh start. By then, we should know what's going on back home and be able to move somewhere more permanent. That way when you start in a school, we know you can stay there. Since that was the main reason we did the homeschool thing this year anyway. You know, to avoid having to switch schools while we moved around." I fastened my eyes back on him. "How does that sound?"

"I'd like that." His lips thinned into a straight line, hinting he was holding back a grin.

When we arrived at the house, Mrs. Michael was sitting at the table, working on a crossword puzzle. She forbade a traditional greeting. "What is a six-letter word that means wiggle, but it's not wiggle?"

I grimaced as it was too early for that much brain work, but Josiah was intrigued, gravitating toward her, and offered, "Fidget."

"You would know that word," I teased as he never sat still long.

"No, I thought of that too," Mrs. Michael replied with a thoughtful tone, "but the last letter has to be an M."

"How about squirm?" Josiah suggested.

"Hmm." She plotted out the letters with a pleased grin growing on her face. "That works." Her eyes raised above the rim of her glasses to Josiah, who was looking over her shoulder at the next clue on the crossword puzzle. She tapped the empty chair next to her. "Have a seat. We have work to do."

He flashed a look at me, as if he was requesting permission, and I smiled back at him until he relaxed into the chair. It was endearing how he had warmed up to her, and I didn't mind if they wanted to entertain each other. Mrs. Michael dropped her eyes to the crossword puzzle and carried on. "What is a seven-letter word that means happy?" Before anyone could respond, footsteps barreled down the steps and Tonya fled out the door, without uttering a word in our direction. Trey was fast behind her but halted his steps when he saw she had already slammed the door. He turned on his heel, with his brow lowered, hinting to how he felt. The silence lingering in the air was so thick it was suffocating.

Desperate to create a distraction, I picked up my extra smoothie shaker and offered it to him. "Here, I made you a smoothie this morning."

He eyed the cup suspiciously. "Why?"

I shrugged, playing down my gesture. "I was making them and figured you could use one too, especially with this week being so huge for you. I put some extra stress support supplements in there." I pushed the cup farther toward him. "Try it."

"And by stress support, do you mean Maalox?" His lips stretched into an even smile, but it didn't reach his eyes.

I snickered, trying to lighten the mood. "No, just some herbs, but I can put that on the grocery list if you need it."

"I should be fine." He sighed like he was lugging around the weight of the world on his back and took a small swig, appearing to swish it around his mouth once before swallowing it. "Not terrible."

"Thank you." I felt like I had scored a double win as he liked my recipe, and he was now distracted from whatever just happened.

Mrs. Michael peered down at Trey through her glasses which were on the tip of her nose. "What do you have going on today, dear?"

He kept his eyes low, focused on the open lid of his smoothie shaker. "Drinks with Allen again. He's wavering."

"What time is that?" she pressed.

"Later." His cautious eyes rose to her. "Why?"

"I was wondering if Tonya would have time to get back." Her face scrunched, as she clearly wasn't trying to hide her dislike for Tonya. "Isn't she supposed to go with you?"

His eyelids lowered back to the shaker again. "No, she's going back to California for good. We broke up."

Mrs. Michael dramatically flopped her jaw open so wide it reminded me of an impressionist painting of a largemouth bass I had seen. I instantly got uncomfortable. *I want out of the aura of this conversation now!* Stumbling over my feet backward, I eased my way to the broom closet and quietly started to yank out my supplies, but I couldn't plug my ears fast enough and I heard her ask, "Doesn't she know you need her this week?"

"Yes." His voice was laced with disappointment. "We talked about it. We've *been* talking about it for weeks. Now we both just knew."

"Well." Mrs. Michael's tone pitched higher than usual like it was suffering from shellshock. "Did you want me to go with you so I can talk to Jane?"

He chuckled but not in an amused way. "I remember the last time you came to talk to Jane. Remember how you offended her by constantly interrupting her?"

"That wasn't intentional. I kept randomly remembering things that were more interesting than what she was talking about."

Trey maintained a straight face. "I'll be fine."

"I don't know about that." Her pitch took on more urgency. "You know how she is. If she isn't the center of attention, she wants to leave immediately."

"I know," Trey's took an even more disgruntled tone. "Atalie found that out the other day. Jane was ready to leave, and if it wasn't for Atalie showing her the art collection, she would have convinced Allen to bail early too."

I should have run out of the door while I had the chance, but I saw it coming in slow motion when Mrs. Michael's posture straightened in exclamation like she had the best idea ever. "Well, then maybe she can go with you tonight?"

"Can't," I immediately declined, letting my eyes slide to Josiah. "I have a kid, remember?" I was one hundred percent sure I did *not* want anything more to do with his business affairs. The last time I did that, we ended up standing way too close for way too long in an encounter that left me flushed for days.

Trey shot me an expression that said he was glad I was ducking out so he didn't have to explain to his mom why he couldn't bring his maid to dinner. "Don't worry about it. I can manage." His voice was firm while he took a few steps down the hall before his phone chimed, which he immediately took out of his pocket. In a flash of a second later, he muttered, "You have got to be kidding me . . ."

"What happened?" Mrs. Michael called after him, her tone growing even more worrisome.

"Allen canceled."

"Drinks?"

"Everything." His voice was stunned, lingering in the air.

"How?"

"He texted that Jane thinks it's too risky, but he wished me the best of luck."

"He has cold feet." Mrs. Michael drew her brows in before continuing, "He is letting his nerves win."

"So, then what?" Trey flicked his hand up in question. "Make him some chamomile tea?" His eyes sped back to his phone as he swiped his phone screen. "I'm calling him."

Relieved that near miss was over, I quickly crossed the kitchen on my tiptoes. It hadn't been my plan to clean the foyer today, but it was down at the other end of the hall. Which suited my current goal perfectly because it put voice-muffling distance between myself and this conversation. Unfortunately, I could hear his voice from the hall, and he wasn't happy. "I can't believe you would bail on me in a text after I thought we had a deal?"

I power sprayed the frosted windows in the French door, trying to pretend I couldn't hear, but the silence in between Trey's comments was smoldering. Finally, he said, "I need someone with your background on this project lead and you're the one I trust the most. You've done all my other projects with me. It only makes sense." Another pause before adding, "I know that's a lot of money, but Jane didn't even talk to me about it. Tell her it's worth meeting me tonight because I can explain everything, and she wouldn't want to miss the opportunity."

Silence.

"I'm sorry you feel that way too. Is there anything I can do to change your mind?"

Silence.

"I really feel like this is a mistake, but you have to do what you have to do."

Silence.

"Is there any way I can still take you out tonight to explain how I revamped everything and if you hate the idea, we can sit and have drinks?"

Silence.

"No, Tonya isn't available tonight to come along."

Silence.

"Well . . . sure, I can bring someone else."

My spine stiffened with some weird ESP, predicting what was coming next. It was confirmed by the sound of his voice coming in more clearly. Wincing in the same way I do when I step on one of Josiah's LEGO blocks, I turned to confirm my suspicion.

He was standing next to me.

I jerked my hand down the hall toward Josiah, but he ignored my gesture and covered his phone with his hand. "He's asking his wife if she would agree to meet me if you come."

Horrified I was getting dragged into this drama, I put a voice behind my excuse this time. "I'd love to help you, but I have a kid to parent." I pulled my lips into my best impression of a disappointed grin. "So, yeah, bummer but unfortunately, I can't go."

He didn't hear it, though, as he spoke into his phone again. "Oh really." His breath released in one giant puff of air. "That's amazing. Tell her thank you so much and seven is great for us." Then he clicked end on the call and immediately looked at me. "I'm sorry"—he took one direct step forward— "but you met Jane and she is one of those people who can't sit still, especially if she's bored. She wouldn't come unless I brought Tonya." His eyes—clouded with anxiety—traced my face like they were looking for any sign of compassion. "I know it's last-minute, but it'll only be an hour or two."

"Um, well . . ." I scratched my cheek as I tried to figure out a way to tell him he was *crazy*! "Not to put myself down, or anything, but don't you think it's going to look weird if I show up with you? They saw me serve food last week." I lowered my voice to block Josiah from hearing me. "They are going to think you hooked up with your maid."

"Nah." He shook his head, completely dismissing my comment. "They know me. I've done business with them from the beginning, and I've always made friends with all my employees and treated everyone like family."

"And you do know." I held up an inquiring finger to assist the point I was about to make. "That when a boss says they are going to treat you like family, that is code for I'm going to drain every ounce of life from you." Even though he sputtered out a surprised laugh, I felt my brow flatten out, realizing how weird this was, and asked, "Don't you have an assistant who does this sort of thing?"

"Not here. My assistant didn't want to relocate from LA. Most of her work is virtual, and we negotiated her contract to stay there. I haven't had time to staff up here." His eyes stayed locked on mine, but not in the enjoyable way they were the last time we stood this close. This time his eyes held flecks of unease that made me wrench with empathy and I didn't like it. Then he added, "It's not a big deal. Just come and talk to Jane."

"So," I started, my thoughts slower than my words could flow. "That's a lot of pressure, and what happens if she gets bored anyway?"

He threw up one shoulder in a shrug. "At least we tried."

I didn't like how he kept using the word we, like his business was part of my responsibility. Other than a vague Google search I had done, I still didn't know what his business was at this point. He filled in the words I didn't say, "Come for drinks and you don't have to worry about anything. If Jane wants to talk to you, then great. If not, no big deal."

I let my eyes lead back down the hall in the direction of Josiah and I was about to point out *again* that I had parenting to do and couldn't go out, but Trey read my mind and immediately spoke, "My mom can watch Josiah."

I sighed, like I was being put in detention and took a few hard steps down the hall until I was able to see Mrs. Michael and Josiah still sitting at the table, working a crossword puzzle together like there was nowhere else either one of them would rather be. The scene was so perfectly ill-timed to fight against my argument that it could have been a commercial! Both Mrs. Michael's head and Josiah's moved in unison to look at me, and it was obvious they had heard our conversation. I waited for Josiah to complain, but he didn't. Feeling slightly betrayed by him, I asked, "Don't you think it will be late for me to be gone?"

"As long as I don't have to go to bed until you get home, I'm fine with her watching me."

I dramatically mouthed the word "traitor" at him. The humored glare he gave me back was unwavering.

I turned to Mrs. Michael, but she was also wore an overly-eager expression when she commented, “I don’t have anything going on tonight and I’m happy to help out.” Her gaze planted on Josiah. “I can show you how Trey and I used to make the best blanket forts and I’m pretty sure I have some dart guns stashed somewhere.” The excitement flashing on Josiah’s face made me want *that* for him, and I realized the negotiations were over.

I reluctantly dragged my eyes back to Trey in defeat. “No pressure.”

“No big deal.” His voice was smooth now, like he knew I was already in.

“Just this once.”

“Deal,” he said so fast, it was barely recognizable. Then he swapped out his sales pitch voice to one that held more business, “Did you want to take off now, so you can get ready, and we’ll come over at around six thirty? I can drop off Mom and pick you up?”

A cold sweat washed over my lower back. “Nah.” I nervously tugged at my ponytail, trying to sound casual, but my inner panic siren was flashing a red alert! “I-I can come back, and we can leave from here.”

He cocked his head to the side. “Are you sure? It might get late, and Josiah might want to sleep.”

I waved my hand at him in a dismissing way. “Nah, he’s a vampire. Totally allergic to sleep.”

Josiah agreed, “Yep, I hate sleep and you already agreed, Mom, I can stay up until you get home.”

“I did say that,” I agreed a little too quickly and I could see a spark of suspicion in Trey’s eyes, but before he had a chance to disagree, I turned to Josiah and instructed, “Why don’t you grab your stuff, and we’ll head out now since we have to come back.”

Trey silently watched me as I helped Josiah pack his bag. When it was loaded, I ushered us quickly out the door, calling back, “See you later.” With one final glance over my shoulder, I casually asked, “Can you tell me where we are going so, I know how to dress?”

He was looking at his phone now, so I didn't have to see his face when he replied, "Jane likes Mayella's and it's all about Jane." Gulping, panic seeped into my chest. I didn't have anything to wear to a place that fancy, but I also couldn't *admit* that. Now I have to worry about this?

Stupid dinners were never part of the job description!

I fought to remain calm as I turned back to Josiah, wondering if there was a thrift shop or consignment store within walking distance. "Let's get moving. I need to find something to wear."

Maybe Trey was worried I'd show up in my smock, because he immediately arched his brow toward me. "It's a weekday and still early enough you could call the stylist Tonya uses. She can send something over for you within the hour at my expense."

"It's okay . . ." I murmured, because my mind warred between not wanting to admit I didn't have anything fancy all the way to being intrigued and wanting to let a stylist dress me.

"No. I insist. I'll text her your number and you guys can chat."

"Well, I guess . . . Thank you." With that Trey buried his face into his phone.

"Josiah," I called over to him, with a new sense of urgency, knowing the time was ticking away, and I had a ton of getting ready to do. *I didn't even shower yet today!* To my surprise, Josiah followed me without complaint, which was pleasant, but I wasn't fooled. Clearly, it was only because he was excited to forgo his bedtime tonight.

Trey called out while still looking down at his phone, "Take my car. It'll save you so much time."

I started to resist, but he was the one putting me in this time crunch. It only made sense for me to accept his help. "We will do that." He still didn't look up, but I added, "Thank you." Without wasting another minute, I changed directions and scurried to the garage.

NINE

Atalie

"I wonder why chicken nuggets taste so much better when you cook them in the oven than when you microwave them." Josiah pondered as we returned to Trey's house.

I wasn't versed in microwave science and rarely used it, but there had been a time, or two, that I'd admit to making nuggets there. "I'm not sure, but you can ask them."

His brow furrowed when he squared his face with mine. "Mom, you can't ask a chicken nugget."

"Maybe you just don't speak their language," I teased as we let ourselves in while I carried my single sack of groceries to the kitchen. Mrs. Michael was in her usual spot at the table, doing another crossword puzzle. This time instead of calling out a clue she was stuck on, she raised her head and properly greeted Josiah. "Hey Josiah, are you ready to build your fort?"

"Yeah, I brought my walkie-talkies."

I set out Josiah's snacks on the counter for easy access while explaining my dinner selection, "I got chicken nuggets, strawberries, and a Caesar salad kit so he gets something sort of healthy for dinner because I didn't have time to make anything." I put the nuggets and salad in the fridge and took a minute to go through the old containers of takeout while calling back out of the fridge, "Unless you have other plans for dinner, but he can be sort of picky."

"I can handle a picky little boy."

"Are you talking about me again?" Trey answered as he bounded down the stairs and emerged wearing a navy suit. I could tell without even touching it that it was expensive fabric. I'm not sure why, but it sent a wave of flutters into the pit of my stomach, and I was glad I had ditched the Alice sneakers for heels. Backing out of the fridge, I slowly shut the door, feeling too exposed. Wearing the dress Tonya's stylist had lent me, I felt prepared for the dinner, but I oddly found myself wondering what Trey thought of how I looked, and my anxiety made it hard for me to make eye contact with him.

"Not this time." Mrs. Michael's voice came out with a humored inflection.

Trey hardly glanced in my direction as he put on an all-business expression and looked to his mom. "Is everybody good here? I don't want to risk being late."

Mrs. Michael waved him out the door. "You two go ahead and leave. We are about to set up our bird watching station."

Josiah's face beamed with anticipation when I leaned in and gave him a hug and kiss goodbye. "Be good. Love you."

"Bye, Mom." He barely looked at me and I took that as a good sign and left with Trey.

As we headed out the door, I whispered, "When this event is over, I expect employee of the month status and a unicorn parade on my behalf."

The smile he cracked was more disbelieving than inviting so I figured he wasn't in the mood to chat. It wasn't until we were down the block that he said, "I think my mom was looking forward to this evening. It's been a long time since she had to entertain a little boy."

"I can see how she might feel a little nostalgic about it. Kids grow up so fast. One minute they are your best friend. Then the next minute, they are too busy to return your phone calls."

"In my case, I don't have to return her phone calls as she doesn't give me the chance. She just comes over." His tone oscillated between forced light-heartedness and apprehensiveness.

I turned, observing him. "Have you two always been close?"

"I don't know if you'd say we're close now."

I gave him my best you-can't-kid-me face. "She comes over every day and is usually there longer than I am, and I'm a full-time employee."

"Right." He tilted his head to the side, then said in a softer voice, "It's difficult with her because she was a single mom. Like Josiah's, my dad also passed when I was young and so after that, it was always just the two of us. She made a lot of sacrifices for me. I always promised to be there to take care of her and I intend to."

Racking my brain, I tried to remember telling Trey my husband had passed, but there was no way I would have let that detail slip out. I hated talking about my personal life and there was only one way for him to know that detail. His mom. It didn't surprise me she had shared that with him, but it made my throat tight when I squeaked out, "Your mom knows a lot about your business."

"I suppose it could look weird to some people, but I had bad luck finding business partners I can trust. I'm careful with who I talk to about things, and I figure if I can't trust my mom, who can I trust?" He was silent for a while before adding, "However, it can be a little much when she comes over every day. She never even asks if I'm busy."

I was completely joking when I offered a solution, "Hmm, if you don't want her there, you could always offer to take her out to lunch and then just drive her home, so she gets the message."

The corner of his lips bent up, teasing a smile. "Just drive her home. Problem solved."

"That should be easy, right?" I tilted my head, bringing my point home.

"In other words, I should take her to lunch every day?""Or better yet, make it breakfast," I joked.

He removed one hand off the steering wheel and thoughtfully added, "I'll have to try that." When he looked at me, his face bore a mischievous grin I had never seen before. "Maybe I'll drop her off at your house and Josiah can keep her busy building blanket forts."

He was joking, but it made me smile because Josiah would love that. "I might actually keep her because if she did that, I could get so much done."

"It's settled then." He tapped the steering wheel like he was confirming a deal. "We are officially sharing custody. I'll take her for an hour for breakfast and you get everything else."

"That's like ninety-ten custody. I'm going to need some parental support at that ratio."

"Take whatever you need." He pretended to give me an imaginary wallet. "As long as everyone can be happy. That's all I want."

Even though we were joking, it felt as if there was a lot of truth in his last words, like he had a kind heart, and he really was trying to make everyone happy. We had arrived at the restaurant, and Trey had once again swapped out his joking expression to his serious look when he looked over at me. "Are you ready for this?"

I forced an all-in smile to put him at ease when I pulled on the door handle and echoed, "Ready."

Ten

Atalie

Trey cased the restaurant as we followed the hostess to our reserved seating in the back corner. I slid into my shoulder-to-shoulder chair with Trey at a table for four. Every few minutes, Trey would crane his neck up to see if he saw them, then his Adam's apple would bob as he put his chin down to look back at the menu. With only ten items on the menu, it should have taken only a couple of minutes to decide what to order, so the amount of time we spent staring at our menus was super awkward. I stole a peek at him to see what he was doing, and it was the exact moment he had chosen to look at me. We both knew we had fallen into a silent rut. I smiled, a little shyly because I wasn't sure if he was uncomfortable sitting with me or just nervous about his meeting. "So," I started, "how did you meet Allen and Jane?"

His eyes fled to the left like he was pulling up a memory. "When I was a freshman in high school, I was hired as an intern on a coding project. They were the lead consultants on it and we just clicked. I didn't have the formal education to secure a job as a coder, but I have a photographic memory and can learn stuff quickly. They mentored me and brought me into other projects." He paused for a second, took a sip of his water, then continued,

"Those two had all these ideas for projects as it was during the dotcom boom and there was easy money. They didn't have the time to code all their ideas. So, they put up the money and I would sit up all night and code. We started with a program for hotels, and that sold and made them both wealthy. Then we wrote a program for builders, and we kept it going. Some programs sold and some didn't. I pretty much spent my twenties in a studio apartment, over juiced on energy drinks and lost in code."

"So, your business now is mostly software?" I tried not to sound too nosey because I knew from my previous life that a lot of rich people didn't like to disclose information with people who weren't business contacts.

"My software company is my biggest asset, but I dabble in investing in other businesses, mostly SPAC. I also consult for startups." He gestured to me with an opened palm. "I'm sure this is all boring for you."

I had no idea what SPAC was, but I didn't want to sound stupid. "No, not at all."

I was about to ask him something else to keep the conversation rolling, but he abruptly stood, announcing, "Here they are."

Jane took the seat in front of me, and when she pulled off her high-collar coat, she unveiled layers of pearls and a white sleeveless shell for a shirt. Even with the overdone bedazzlement, she looked radiant. Without wasting a moment, she leaned over the table to greet me. "Nice to see you again . . ." Her Botoxed brows held a pause in my direction like she was waiting for me to complete her thought. My apprehension about being *just the maid* left me with a serious case of imposter syndrome and I found myself wondering if this is how Cinderella might have felt.

"Atalie," Trey said softly, finishing her sentence when I was unable to come up with my own reply. My eyes sped to his, and he held my gaze gently, like he was letting me know I had his support.

"Ah." Jane's vibrant blue eyes popped wider as she leaned closer to me and proclaimed in a loud voice, "Like Natalie without the N, right?"

Swallowing my nervous tension as best I could, I replied, “Yes, exactly like that.”

“I’d apologize for being late but I’m not really sorry,” she blurted out. I thought she was joking, so I started to laugh but she breezed right into her next sentence, and I could tell she was serious about not being sorry. “I had to rescue a cat stuck underneath my dryer.”

“Oh no,” I empathized. “That doesn’t sound good. Did you get him out?”

“Yes, he hides under there when the females are being bullies. He’s the sensitive type.”

I overheard Trey ask Allen about some report and I realized that was the formal hand-off. I was officially going to have to keep this cat conversation going by myself. Leaning back in my chair, I dove further into the cat chat, “So . . . do you have a lot of cats?”

Taking a moment to brush a piece of her *straight as straw, salt and pepper* hair that had stuck to her lip back neatly behind her ear, she leaned forward even more. “Well, I rescue them, so right now I have a few dozen.”

“Wow.” I blinked dramatically at the visual.

“I know.” She nodded at me in a reassuring way. “It’s a little overwhelming. I bought a three-bedroom home and remodeled the basement just for the cats.”

There must have been a pause in Trey’s conversation because they overheard the last part of Jane’s comment. Allen flicked his eyes to land on mine. “That’s what you do when you have too much money. You buy buildings to put cat trees in.”

“Right.” I sheepishly smiled at Jane, a little afraid of her since learning she was basically the definition of a crazy cat lady. When the waiter came back, Jane spoke for me by saying, “She needs to try the wine-infused pasta with clams.” Her eyes were on the waiter, but her finger pointed sharply at me.

I had a *slight* issue, so I squeaked out, “Well, I can do pasta . . . that sounds good.” I made a squeamish look at Jane and voiced my correction. “However, I’m allergic to seafood, so can I have chicken?” I gritted my teeth into a toothy grin, feeling Jane’s eyes on me.

The waiter nodded, completed our orders, and left, leaving me exposed so I hopped back on the cat-chat train. She spoke rapidly and bounced from one story to the next. I wasn’t sure what she was talking about, but I kept smiling as she carried on about her cats, their relationships, medical issues, and just about everything you can think of. When a pause came in Trey and Allen’s conversation, Trey asked how it was going on our end of the table, and Jane spoke for me, “It’s going well, but this one”—she nodded in my direction— “sure doesn’t talk much.”

My cheeks boiled, feeling defensive as I hadn’t had a chance to talk! I toyed with the idea of following the waiter to the back room and tipping him twenty bucks to spill a glass of wine all over me so I’d have a solid excuse to leave, but the less sane part of me couldn’t do that to Trey. One bonus, though, her constant chatter made it easy for me to eat my meal because I only had to make sure I had a pleasant look on my face and kept eye contact with her while I chewed. I also threw in a nod every time she broke out into laughter over her own comment. It wasn’t as bad as . . . say, dying would be, but it made for a long night.

When Trey finally paid the bill, I fought like crazy to hold back a sigh of relief. Jane leaned in for a hug and squeezed me like she’d been training for the all-American strong hug team. Trey had a humored grin on his face, busting him for the fact he had prior knowledge of her super squeezy strength.

As soon as they were out the door, Trey emitted the explosive sigh I had been holding in. I meekly slumped back down in my chair, matching his mood. Instead of talking, we fell into a silence, and I stared back at him, noting his eyes were more steel-colored than I had remembered—but I imagined it was because of the mellow glow from the light above us. His eyes seemed to burn with disgust and his lips were sealed tight and straight.

I didn't have a clue what to say to him. I was supposed to be just his housekeeper—who had fantastic hair—but even the amazing hair part had to get rewritten, thanks to his possessed paper shredder.

His eyes flicked back to the table, landing on his wallet which had been left out. He picked it up, flashing it at me, and with a tiny curl from a corner of his lips, he said, "How big of a tip do I owe you? I'm pretty sure I heard cat poop at least twelve times."

I chuckled, letting my eyes draw to his. "I honestly didn't hear that part. I zoned out and started planning my unicorn parade."

Parting his lips, as if he was going to talk, he surprised me when he didn't say anything. Instead, he held his eyes locked on mine. This wasn't his all-business look, but it was something similar to what happened the other night and the energy behind his gaze sent a shot of adrenaline right to my core. It was so potent it sent fizzy bubbles to my stomach that sparked like Pop Rocks. They were obviously mobile and traveled up my throat, tightening my vocal cords. Thankfully, he abruptly stood, saving me from my crazy bubbling spiral when he said, "It's getting late, and Josiah is waiting for you."

The night's energy felt worn out and I didn't even try to talk. We made it all the way across the parking lot in silence. When Trey opened my car door, he stood back, waiting for me to get in. He smiled and held my eyes. "I noticed you left your old-lady sneakers at home."

I held my best messing-with-you-straight face. "I like to wear heels when I hang out with new people because if they turn out to be creeps, I can always use my shoe as a weapon and throw it at them."

He rubbed the back of his head, letting his hand hook on his neck. "Good to know."

"You've been warned."

His lips curved into a thin smile, and I sank back into my seat. I was so sick of conversation after Jane's nonstop ramblings I was ready to relax in the silence as he drove home.

Eleven

Trey

It was all over Allen's face the moment he walked in that he was done helping me, but I couldn't give up and let my project fold. It wasn't even the money, because I had more than enough passive income to live on forever, but I *knew* all the people who worked in my software division. They'd worked for me for years and felt like an extended family. Not to mention they needed their jobs. I had a whole team who worked on this app for over a year—everyone from programmers to a top-notch marketing team. There were always other capital firms I could seek out, but this wasn't about the money. It was about putting a person I trusted in charge, and Allen was my most trusted partner.

To top it off, Atalie kept looking at me with this sweet expression full of empathy. There was *something* effortless about hanging out with Atalie. She was quiet when I needed to think, attentive when I needed to talk, and optimistic when I needed to vent my stress. I hated my mind went there, but it was different than when I was with Tonya.

Tonya had a way of making me feel like I wasn't enough for her. I couldn't even blame it on being rich. When I traced through my memories, it had always been like that. I always felt like I had to chase after her. In the beginning, it gave me a rush. She was a little manic and I thought it was exciting. After all of the years, it had become exhausting. I'd admit I often wondered what it would be like to have a partner who would be happy to just *be* there for me in the same manner I was happy to be there for her. It was a pointless thought which I pushed out of my head and went for easy conversation. "I texted my mom to let her know we're on our way. We should be able to grab Josiah and I'll take you both home."

Atalie shifted her legs like she was tensing up. "That's fine. You don't have to give us a ride home." Her face was pinched like something was bothering her. I had seen that exact expression the last time I had offered to drive her home. I'd assumed it was because she was embarrassed for me to see where she lived, but like I cared about that? This was arguably one of the most expensive states to live in and she was raising a son on her maid's salary. I would never judge her for that.

I didn't want her to feel bad, or pry into her personal life so I made a different offer. "Maybe I can get you a set of keys to my car for these sort of nights." I looked over at her—accidentally noticing the streetlights did a phenomenal job at illuminating the side of her face. Other than the day I got to study the top of her head, I hadn't really looked at her before tonight, but I found it hard to pull my eyes away. Her raven-dark hair contrasted to her ivory skin, and her dramatic green eyes seemed to change colors at least twice in the few minutes we'd been sitting here. She had one of those smiles that seemed so sweet and shy, like it could never utter a negative word, but when paired with her eyes, I'd bet she wasn't as innocent as she looked. At first glance, she was gorgeous, but it was a different kind of beauty than you see in magazines. She fell more into the stunning, hot mess category.

"I hope it doesn't become a pattern," she quipped, but the expression on her face was pleasant and not at all displeased.

I tossed a shoulder up and spoke my thoughts as they came. "Or maybe I can let you have a car as an employee benefit."

Her eyes latched on me, but I stayed focused on the road and didn't look over. I was serious about the offer but still felt vulnerable to her response. Instead of replying to my suggestion, a smile sparked her lips. "Purple is my favorite color."

"For a car?"

"No, for my parade."

"You do know . . ." My words were slow, hinting of bad news. ". . . that unicorns aren't a real thing?"

She playfully pushed her hand out like she didn't want to hear it. "Just because you're a boring old guy who believes only the things you see exist, doesn't mean there isn't magic in the unseen."

I rubbed my chin with my hand, wondering how far she would take this stupid unicorn thing. I couldn't help but think it was a little silly. Is she even remotely serious? Maybe it's because she hangs out with her son all day and she's forgotten what normal adults talk about? It seemed odd to think about, but I ranted in my head the whole way back to my house, and I realized I hadn't thought about Allen or the shadows on Atalie's face.

So maybe I didn't hate unicorns . . .

It was a new day, and I had a new idea.

I was going to save my company.

I had the money to take it forward by myself, but I needed to find another project leader who had the vision. Lucky for me, I knew just the man who could help me.

Evan would be an obvious choice, but he only worked until noon every day and I needed someone who could handle the long hours. I thought about another buddy from college, and like the rest of us—a genius in coding, but he had a few quirks.

Maybe not a few, but one challenging one.

He talked like Donald Duck.

I could only understand about every other thing he said, especially when he got excited or upset. He'd slur his words together and all you'd hear was a crackling swishing noise that sounded like an upset washing machine. But he had a heart of gold. I'd never met anyone with a more generous heart than him. I couldn't even count the times he gave his last few dollars to a random charity can collecting coins or wrapped up his leftovers when he was still hungry and handed them out to a street beggar. He'd never say no to me, especially after I told him how many people were about to lose their jobs.

There was only one sort of negative thing about it.

Although he was a programmer and impressive with technology, he didn't have a phone because he lived in Indonesia, and not like one of its notable cities. Yeah, I glossed over that last part for a reason. He had gotten recruited as a missionary to work in the isolated swamplands. No internet. No electricity. Totally off-grid. Told ya—heart of gold.

I emailed him, requesting a meeting, and offered to come to his neck of the . . . swamp. Due to limited email access, it took a week for him to get back to me, and lucky me, he replied with an eager invite to visit *this* weekend and news of his recent engagement. He was excited for me to meet his fiancée, a lovely Asmat woman. Although, he warned me that their engagement was still a secret because he feared her brothers would beat him up if they found out. Oh, and he requested I bring Tonya so our girlfriends could meet. Even if we hadn't broken up, Tonya was a high-maintenance princess. Not a girl you could take to a swamp.

Feeling slightly defeated, I closed my laptop, as well as my eyes, hating what I was about to do. I loathed asking for help, especially after what I'd been through this last year. It was painful to have to rely on someone else, but I knew Robert well and since he saw my depression last year, he would need to see my life was stable before he would commit to helping me. He would find my recent breakup with Tonya alarming and worry about my mental health. I had to convince him I was in a good place.

Rubbing my chin, I mused the best way to do that was to prove I had moved on . . .

Cringing slightly, I reopened my laptop, feeling badd*ish* for not asking first. I felt it was one of those minor logistical things that didn't always have to happen in proper order. Before I let the moral part of my brain convince me it wasn't the most appropriate thing to sign up my newest employee for, I emailed back.

Robert- Congrats on your engagement. You lucky dog. Can't wait to meet her. Tonya and I broke up, but don't worry, I met someone else who would love to come.

See ya on Saturday,

Trey

Before I lost my momentum, I headed upstairs where I found Atalie. She caught my eyes before I could speak. Even though she did turn toward me, she took a significant step back, placing her in the corner. "Hear me out," I led, which I found out wasn't the best way to open a conversation.

"Not interested," she said flatly, folding her arms across her chest.

I tried a different approach, one that would make her feel sorry for me as I continued to pace toward her, halting my steps an appropriate arm's reach away from her. "So, I made a mistake."

"Then say you're sorry." Her eyes looked past me like they were searching for the closest fire exit.

I took another step closer, boxing her in the corner. Never thought about corners before, but I decided I loved them. They created such a lovely backdrop for trapping people. "One more meeting."

"You said it was just one meeting to begin with."

"Right. That was with Allen, and he bailed. Now I need to meet with a different friend."

Her eyes bounced around my face, making me wonder if she could tell how much I was withholding. Luckily, I prided myself on being a champion at staring contests and I held my gaze steady.

"Do you need me to go on another dinner?" she asked.

I chin nodded my way through the words. "Something like that, sure."

Her inquiring eyes washed over my face again, like she was searching for clues. "It is, or it isn't?"

"It is," I said firmly.

Her eyes narrowed. "Then why are your eyes so shifty?"

"They aren't shifty." I willed my eyes to freeze in place. "They are sensitive."

Her tiny nostrils flared slightly as she drew in a loud breath, and in a voice that seemed to hold more amusement than annoyance, she said, "I'm not going to be your work wife, if that's what you think. This has got to stop."

"One more time."

"I don't even know what you're asking."

Right. She needed details.

In a rush, I blew through the specifics, hoping she wouldn't get a chance to actually hear any of it. "We fly to an Indonesian mangrove swamp, and we paddle a canoe upriver where we'll camp in a cozy hut. Fly home the next day." I felt it was wise to leave out the part about the famous disappearance of that Rockefeller guy and a sprinkling of archeologists. Pfft. Minor details she didn't need to know.

That she can read about on the internet!

Note to self: send a disabling virus to all her internet devices. *Today.*

Atalie's eyes grew freakishly large. "Ah, that's a hard no! When I said I would work hard for you in my job application, I didn't mean I would *die* for you."

Okay, maybe she wasn't going to be so easy to convince. I decided to take a different approach. "How about a raise?"

"You couldn't pay me enough." Her words came out broken through a sarcastic chuckle.

"A year off . . . paid?"

"Deal. I'll start today." She pushed a flattened palm just inches in front of my chest and ducked to the left like she was going to leave. I used this perfect right-angled gift to my advantage and took yet another step closer. I was so close; I could smell her skin—it was sweet.

Like honey. Maybe a touch of tropical.

Man, she smelled amazing.

A little enchanted.

Stop! Don't get distracted.

To stop my scrolling thoughts, I blurted out, "It's only one night there."

"Yeah," she continued in her skeptical tone, "how long does it take to get there?"

"A day or so." I downplayed the details by tossing up a shoulder and casually gesturing forward. "Consider it a long weekend."

"I'm not a criminologist, but I'm pretty sure that's what human traffickers say."

I'll give her that one. That was a pretty good comeback. "I already said you would go. If I go back on my word now, that makes me a liar."

"That sort of sounds like asking first."

"I figured you'd enjoy getting out of the house for a few days."

"Not happening."

"Why not?"

"I'm allergic to it."

Her lips were strained, and I could tell she was fighting back a laugh. I was slowly winning her over. I bantered back, "You can't be allergic to a vacation."

She rebutted with, "That's not a vacation."

"It'll be nice to get away for a couple of days."

"I have Josiah—"

I cut her off, "My mom will watch him."

Her eyes flickered in a way that told me she had a new idea, and that was confirmed when she asked, "Why don't you just take your mom?"

"Well . . ." I bobbed my head back and forth, weighing the risk of what I was about to say, "I can't . . . I sort of need to make Robert believe we are *together.*"

Her eyes snapped back at mine so fast I thought I heard a whip crack. "What?"

"So funny thing . . . I need him to trust that I'm not going to screw everything up like I did last year when I was depressed. He isn't going to believe me that I'm not all sad over my breakup with Tonya. I wanted to try to show him I moved on with someone else . . ." Then I pushed my hand out, waving it in a no, and rushed to add, "Don't worry. There will be *nothing weird* between us. Just show up and everything will be very professional still—"

Her head took a side angle when she cut me off, "What, wait, say that again?"

"I ah, sort of need you to pretend that we're *together.*"

Her shoulders rose slowly, and her eyes steadied, trapping mine. I waited for her excuse, but she never refuted so I confirmed in a soft voice, "So, we are good to go then?"

"No!" her head snapped back like she had been startled out of a daydream. "No, we are not *good to go!* What if something bad happens? That's too far to be away."

"Nothing bad will happen."

Her voice was unwavering when she stated, "I can't."

"You can wear your pointy shoes and stab me if you hate it."

"Good, I'll go get them right now." She sidestepped, trying to pass around me again, but I was swift and snatched her forearm, holding her back.

"Come on, Atalie, we both know how this ends."

She was an expert face contortionist because one of her eyebrows arched above the other while the other eye lowered. Her voice rolled out in a low tone, "What do you mean we both know how this ends?"

I dropped her arm, letting my own arm fall back to my side. "It means . . . That you are too nice to say no, and eventually, you'll give in once I find your price. Tell me your price and we can save a lot of time. Is there anything you want?"

Her eyes clung to mine like they were testing me when she echoed, "Anything?"

I could tell she was thinking by the lines stacked on her forehead all the way to her widow's peak. I had hit a nerve. "Anything you can dream of that money can buy."

Something must have been on her mind because without pause she said, "I want access to your lawyers at your expense."

"My lawyers?" It was such an odd request my thoughts got gnarled up like the mangroves we were about to explore. "Are you in legal trouble?"

"And you can't ask questions about it."

"My lawyers specialize in business law." I quirked a brow as this was getting interesting. "Are you wanting to start a business?"

She held up her index finger and repeated, "No questions."

"I don't know what to say about that."

"You can say we have a deal."

Somehow, she had taken control of the conversation, and I was the one left stuttering, "Well, yeah. But—" My mind was a battle zone, with one side begging me to agree because that would mean she'd go, but the other side was vastly curious wanting to know more.

"But what?"

"But it's weird."

"You're asking me to get on a plane—just the two of us." She flattened a palm defensively on her chest. "Fly halfway across the world to some swamp land and you think I'm offering the weird deal?"

"I mean, when you put it that way . . . They are probably equal in weirdness."

"This is your offer to lose." She let the last word dangle on her tongue like she was about to rescind the offer.

I didn't take the chance. "I'll forward your info to my lawyers and have them get in touch with you." I thought she'd respond with something sassy, but instead, she did a final eye sweep across my face before leaving with a serious expression.

Then I reflected on what had just happened.

I had convinced Atalie to go away with me for the weekend. I didn't know why it felt like my heart was beating in random compartments of my chest faster than regular speed, but I knew I didn't hate swamps.

Twelve

Atalie

A long flight into the capital city and several guided boat rides later, our guide left us standing on a deserted shoreline of the river to complete the final leg of the trip—*alone.* It shouldn't have been hard, but it's not like Google Maps worked here. I scanned the terrain, noting the palm trees and dense forestation which appeared exactly how it had looked when I searched online. That part didn't bother me because it was very beautiful. The thing that made my gut squirm was seeing how deserted this part of Indonesia was. "Are you sure you have the directions memorized?" I asked Trey again as I watched our tour guide's raft get smaller as he navigated back up stream, away from us.

"Yeah, I didn't have any paper, so I wrote it on my arm. That way I can't lose it." As if to reassure me, he held up his arm, flashing the inside for me to see his neat boxy penmanship. Revealing a new wave of tan from the boat ride, he obviously had olive-toned skin which tanned easily and didn't burn, unlike my fair skin that forced me to reapply sunscreen every hour. Surprisingly his arm was toned and sinewy, not what I would expect from a guy who coded for a living. My nervous eyes paced the directions, ensuring I didn't see anything wrong with them.

I tugged at my backpack, adjusting the straps for the zillionth time with the quiver in my stomach starting to rumble. I had been doing mostly *okay* because we had our guide, but this was different. This was eerie. Quiet. Well, not totally silent. I could hear the water sloshing along the shore in a relaxed pattern and some random hissing noises springing from the tall grasses. *Grasshoppers.* I told myself.

"Okay." I turned to him, latching my eyes with his. There was a seriousness in his gaze telling me he was also alert, but not fearful. "What's the plan?"

He motioned to the shoreline downstream to where a canoe rested. "We walk this way, grab the boat Robert left for us, and paddle downstream, around a bend, take the left fork, and stop at the village."

Rolling my shoulders to get them to loosen up, I breathed measured breaths. "That shouldn't be too bad."

"Yeah"—he took a step forward leading the way— "we stay on this path and keep your eyes open."

"It looks like the water is flowing enough for it to push us gently too," I added, pretending I knew something about riding dilapidated boats in crocodile-infested water.

"It's doing alright for now, but the guide said the tide will wash back in the next couple of hours, and we don't have time to waste."

"Such a lovely ray of sunshine with your good news all of the time," I said sarcastically as we butted up next to the boat. Now that we were this close, it looked more like a giant piece of tree bark than anything that could pass for a boat. Another rumble of anxiety pumped through my veins. Casting my eyes downriver, I still couldn't see any humans, so I nervously clenched Trey's arm as he pulled the small boat into the water.

When he looked back at me with a stoic expression, my gut twisted in the same manner it did when I watched horror movies. His lips parted in pause, and when he didn't strap a smile on his lips, I saw something was wrong. "What is it?" I winced through narrow eyes, afraid of the worst. Shoot, out here I was afraid of the best.

"There are no oars."

"What!" I threw my gaze back to shore, scanning along the grass. "There has to be something."

He scratched the back of his head, hinting at his own nervousness. "Maybe they washed away, or someone took them?"

"How do we get new ones?"

"I mean, we could totally try Cabela's if you want."

I gave him my best not-funny glare. "You're hilarious."

"Well, look around a bit. Maybe we can find a flat stick or something?" He took a few steps back up toward the tall grass.

I gnawed on my bottom lip, still clenching Trey's lower arm as we made a pass through the grass in search of anything that would save us. There was no way I was going to risk having him ditch me. "Do you have practice being a superhero?"

Leaving his feet planted firmly on the path, he turned his upper body and looked at me flatly in the eyes. "What?"

"I feel like that's what we're missing," I nervously rambled. "That or Rambo."

"No, we're missing the oars. Let's not get carried away."

"Right? I wouldn't want to get carried away . . . By a croc or anything else."

"Will you stop?"

"I think we need to go back to the last village. I had no idea it would be this desolate and we don't even have life jackets." I nervously turned my head back, hoping to catch a glimpse of our tour guide still floating upstream, but unfortunately, there was no evidence he had ever been there. *We are alone.*

"We can't paddle upriver without oars, and our guide won't be back until tomorrow. We obviously don't want to camp out here in the wild, so our only option is to move toward the village."

I used my nervous singsong voice to fill in the quiet air and sang out, "I don't see any sticks."

Trey appeared to do one final scan of the terrain before stopping his steps. "Me neither."

"What do we do now?" I gazed up at him from my permanent spot of being attached to his arm. It was a nice arm. Like something a crocodile would enjoy snacking on. Much weightier than mine. Maybe I could take solace in that?

Trey interrupted my thoughts by asking, "Ah, what do you have in your bag?"

"Let me check." I slipped it off my shoulder, dropped it on the ground, and unzipped it. "I wasn't going to take any chances on the food here, so I have twenty-two protein bars, three liters of water, and a change of clothes. Oh, and three bottles of sunscreen," I reported when I looked back at him. "How 'bout you?"

"Three bags of jerky, water, and clothes."

A new layer of fear washed over me. An ice layer, cooling my lower back despite the scorching temps. "What are we going to do?"

With a degree of assertion, he reached his hand forward. "Give me your bag?"

"Why?" I asked, while clenching the bag protectively.

"I'm going to combine our items into one and use the other as a paddle." He studied my bag for a minute. "Mine looks to be more waterproof than yours so we'll use that for a paddle and take our stuff in yours."

"Aren't you a Boy Scout?" I relented and opened my bag, squashing the contents down to make room for Trey's things, but there wasn't much room left, especially with the giant bottles of water. "I don't think we have room for yours."

"Here." He reached forward again, waiting for me to hand over my bag. "We are going to have to leave some stuff behind."

"Not the water or food." I glared back at him as I slowly passed my bag over.

"No, I agree we bring all the water and food we can." He dug his hand in my bag, pushing the waters back to see how much room he could create. Then he pulled out my sunscreen bottles. "You only need one of these."

"Fine, but where are we going to leave it?"

"I guess we can set it back on the shore and if it's still here when we get back, we'll grab it."

"Do you know the punishment for littering in an Indonesian swamp?"

"No, do you?"

"No, but something tells me they don't take Visa."

"Good thing I mostly have crypto." He pushed the sunscreen bottles back at me. "We have already wasted too much time looking for the oars and we need to get in the boat before the tide recedes and we are stuck." The look he gave me burned and not in a good way. He hurriedly dug his hand back into my bag, pulled out my clothes, and pushed them over to me. "Here, put these somewhere."

My eyes fell over my clothes. Not that they were expensive or anything I was attached to, but I wasn't comfortable leaving my clothes out in the wild. Still, I relented and walked them over to the edge of the grass, setting them neatly down. Trey was done zipping my bag up and his bag was empty now. "Here." He reached my bag back to me. "Put this on so it won't accidentally fall off the boat."

"Right. Or when I fall over, it will pull me to the bottom, so I drown."

"Better to drown than be eaten."

"You're such a planner."

We inched closer to the boat, and I asked, "Any last words?"

"Stop," he said in a surprisingly calm voice, before he took my hand, pulling me forward. We silently took our places, kneeling inside the boat with Trey in front. I tried not to notice how far the boat sank with both of us in it, as the top of the sides of the boat were practically level with the water's edge. Another few pounds in this death rocket and it would have filled with water. We were basically in a food trough for crocs.

"I suppose it is too much to ask for a seat belt." I desperately tried to pretend this was something fun, like a ride in a theme park.

"You'll be okay. Just hold on to me."

I carefully balanced my weight as I shimmied up a hair farther to sit right behind him—like motorcycle close now. In any other setting, this would have been exciting to sit so close to a man so handsome, but I was scared rigid and unable to enjoy anything about the moment. My eyes brimmed wide, and my ears were attuned as Trey carefully leaned his long arms over the side of the boat and dragged his backpack through the water like an underwater sail. When I felt the boat propel forward in the water, I let out a breath I didn't even know I was holding.

"Trey," I whispered after we had seemed to get going at a slow but *steady bobbing, yet somehow, miraculously floating* pattern downstream. "I want to put in my notice."

He chuckled for the first time all day, and I felt the edge of my lips tighten, but I was still too scared to risk a smile. "Not accepted."

"No, I'm serious. Did you know it would be this bad when you asked me to come?"

"I mean, I thought we'd have oars, but that's a minor logistical thing."

"If I can't quit, I have a complaint about my hazardous work environment and need to talk to HR."

"I'll get you their number as soon as we get back."

"Like, not even joking a little bit, but I can't die. I have a son to raise, and he already lost one parent—" My voice cracked on the word parent. I wasn't going to get emotional about this in front of Trey but felt he needed to understand how serious this was for my son. I swallowed, trying again, "There's no one else."

He was quiet for a moment before finally speaking in a low voice, "I'm not going to let anything happen to you."

"So, just so we're clear, then."—I sniffed, stifling my sorrow—"Let's say we get into a situation and it's either you or me who must be sacrificed; you just volunteered." I tried to add sarcasm to my tone to lighten my own mood, but I'd admit I was serious about that last part.

"I guess I did, but then you'll be left here alone."

"Right. Bad idea."

"It is a bad idea because you don't need to worry about anything happening."

I watched the river's edge as we drifted, expecting to see huts or canoes or other people around, but it was so isolated, making it maliciously creepy. "They're expecting us, right?" Just then, the boat wobbled, fishtailing the slightest bit as we seemed to have dropped into deeper water. My fists clenched in reflex, and I dug into Trey's sides. Pinching my lips together, I suppressed a scream with my extremities shaking in fear. Trey must have felt my trembling because he reached back until he found my leg and gave it a slight squeeze. It was a friendly pat, totally meant to be reassuring, but it made goosebumps rocket through my body, reminding me of the attraction to him I had been randomly experiencing.

"Relax." His voice was calmer than any person in this situation should be, like we were just going for a stroll over the lake in Central Park. "And to answer your question, yes, they are expecting us."

"Can you remind me again why we are doing this? It seems a little extreme to visit a friend. Can't you find a new friend on Long Island?"

"Okay, I'll admit that I didn't think it would be *this* bad. I thought there'd be more villages and people around. I've traveled a lot and have seen a lot of wild lands, but this is also not what I was expecting, but since we're here . . ."

"Right, because at this point, we don't have a choice."

"Right."

"So, tell me something to keep my mind busy."

"What do you want to hear?"

"Um, explain to me how a coder ends up doing humanitarian work out here?"

"You can ask Robert when we see him, but I don't think there's too much of a story. I think he heard they were looking for missionaries. He was bored of the routine job stuff and saw it as an adventure." He motioned ahead. "I see our village and there are people by the shore."

Even though I wasn't put at total ease, something about seeing other living humans was reassuring. As far as my opinion went, Trey couldn't paddle this little boat fast enough as I studied the huts before us. I didn't know why I was stunned at this point. I had imagined something cute and round, like one of those huts you see on Hawaiian websites. Surprise—not surprise—these were not. A few huts were hanging over the crocodile's mouth—I mean, the water's edge—suspended on what looked like giant tree trunks. However, most of the huts were farther back. A day ago, I would have cried and refused to go into this village, but so much had happened in the last twenty-four hours that these little huts looked welcoming. Okay, not welcoming, but not as deadly as floating on rotted tree bark.

A man who looked like he could be Jack Black's twin, wearing tan shorts and a plain T-shirt, waited on the shore for us, waving us in. I never wanted to hug a stranger so much in my life, and I couldn't stop smiling at him when Trey helped me out of the boat and introduced us, "Robert, this is . . . Atalie. The woman I told you about." Trey's smile held a tinge of unease as he watched me step forward, but I easily greeted Robert with a grin.

Robert took a step forward and shook my hand. "It's a pleasure to meet you, and I'm impressed you made it here."

His words were garbled together, just as Trey had warned me. It was a little like trying to decipher what a toddler was saying, I didn't have too much of a problem following him. "It's nice to meet you, and I'm super impressed with myself too."

Trey's smile spread wide across his face, but he didn't add anything as I clung right to his side, pretending to be *with* him. Robert took his spot as a host, giving us a tour. I was expecting to be calm since I was on solid ground, but a new boulder of anxiety smashed that expectation.

I worried how I would survive spending all this time *with* Trey.

THIRTEEN

Trey

Robert had pointed us in the direction of the huts with an invitation to get settled. Atalie took one look at the little stilted log hut covered with wild moss growing up its walls and fastened her gaze back on me. "Please don't tell me this is where you take all your lady friends?"

"Considering I've had one girlfriend since I was fifteen—and she would have passed out dead the second we got off my plane—no. You're the first lucky lady who gets to stay here." I started to walk forward, but Atalie lagged, more hesitant than me. The hut was surrounded by deep puddles of water, and they could have easily been filled with snakes, critters, or crocs. I knew she was scared but threw out an incentive to get her to move. "Come on, or I'm going to leave you here by yourself."

That did it.

She was back on my arm again.

I was starting to get used to her there too. Like a pirate who carried a parrot around. *A hundred-pound parrot with sharp claws she periodically pierced through my skin, trying to draw all my blood out.*

It's cool, though. I'm tough.

In an Elon Musk sort of way.

With her claws intact, I gritted my teeth and pulled her forward. "Robert said there's a cultural thing where the men sleep separately from the women. I'll stay with the men in their yew, but this is where the women sleep. He said there's an empty bunk in the back you can grab."

"You're leaving me?" Her voice was tiny, and I swore I could hear teeth chattering.

I didn't think I'd ever had a woman look at me more longingly, but it didn't feel special because I knew she was mainly wanting to have a spare body around in case she needed something warm to toss out for croc food. "I'm only going three hundred feet in that direction," I assured her as I motioned to the larger hut farther back into the brush.

"I can't even communicate with anyone but you or Robert. There should be some sort of rule that says we can stay together."

"Okay, I can see you're still nervous." I put my hand over hers, trying to act reassuring, but in truth, it was because I was trying to nonchalantly loosen her death grip on my arm. "I'll go claim a spot to sleep, throw my things down, and I'll meet you back down by the river in a bit. It's almost time for the women to go fishing."

She let out a sarcastic laugh. "You're kidding."

"Nope." I smiled because now that we were safe on land, I enjoyed teasing her. I wasn't doing it to be mean, but her animation was adorable.

"I'll eat my protein bars."

"It might be offensive not to join them."

She shrugged her shoulders, like she was willing to take a chance. "What's the offense?"

I tucked my hands into my pockets and rocked back on my heels. "I mean, they used to be cannibals, but I'm almost sure they forgot how good humans taste by now."

"Why do I feel like I'm in an Agatha Christie novel?"

"Oh, we're past that." I pulled my lips into my best mischievous grin. "We're on Stephan King level stuff now."

"Why do I get the sense you're enjoying this?"

"I don't hate it."

She flicked her eyes heavenward before heading into her hut alone. I had expected her to turn back and say something sassy, but she didn't. Then I found myself wishing she had.

"I thought it was the women's job to fish?" Atalie raised her chin, looking at me as Robert and I jogged to meet her. Surprised she was there, I had half expected her to have a nervous breakdown by this point. Carrying two primitive fishing poles over my shoulder and a small bowl of worms, I stopped next to her and pressed my lips near her ear to whisper, "It's custom, but Robert informed me this is one of the secret ways he gets to spend time with his fiancée."

Her lips made a silent oh and her eyes fled to Robert. I knew which woman was his fiancée because Robert had introduced me a few seconds ago. Now, he walked out in front of the crew, like he was looking for better fishing. The woman he loved was the first lady behind him, pretending to be equally interested in studying the waters for signs of fish. Keeping my voice concealed near her ear, I whispered again, "It's the woman with the longer grass skirt right behind him."

Her lashes seemed to flutter like butterfly wings before she gave me a light toss of the shoulder and said, "Well, let's head out."

I was impressed she wasn't attaching herself to my arm. It felt so light to not have to tow an extra person around. I freely swung my arms and it felt so good. I must have gotten a little excessive in my arm swinging because she bucked an inquiring brow at me. "Why do you look like those wild monkeys?"

"It feels amazing not to drag all that dead weight around."

"I'm not dead—yet."

"It's true. You seem to have relaxed a little." I kept pace right beside her. "Are you feeling better?"

"A little. It helps to be in a community, even if I can't talk to anyone. I'm trying hard not to think about the other stuff."

"That's good to do. You let your mind run crazy on the way over here." I pointed to a tree near the edge of the riverbank, shading the water. "Let's try casting over there."

She followed me down the bank and lowered to her butt to scoot along the rocks down the steepest part. I kept my eyes on her, but she was nimbler now that she wasn't terrified of losing her life, and she did perfectly fine. She stopped at the water's edge, reaching back, she called to me, "Hand me a pole. I think I see something."

I reached the pole I had baited forward. "So, you do fish?"

She took the pole, inspected the hook and worm, then dropped the line straight into the water. "I'm a mom of a little boy. Therefore, I fish."

"Right."

A new look of worry washed over her face. "How do you think they're doing, by the way?"

I slipped a fat worm on the other pole. "I'm sure they are having too much sugar, and he has probably missed a blue smoothie or two, but he might thank me for that."

She flicked her line back up and frowned. "I had a nibble, but he took my worm and sped off." Her eyes studied the water before she reached back. "Hand me the bowl."

Impressed she had requested an entire bowl full of slimy worms, I dropped the center of the bowl right into her cupped palm and watched as she didn't even flinch when she picked up another worm and sliced the hook right through it.

I was intrigued by this sudden new bravery she had. This time, instead of dropping the line straight down, she flung it back over her shoulder in a traditional cast but when she pulled the line forward it wouldn't rebound. The line was stuck in the tree.

"It's okay," I assured her as she tugged on the line impatiently. "I can get it unstuck." I moved toward the tree, but she called over.

"It's not stuck anymore. It came loose." Then, like she had spotted BigFoot standing behind me, her eyes grew so wide—panicked accents flashed alarms at me. She opened her mouth as wide as a foghorn and expelled the most audibly obnoxious screech that seemed to tilt the earth's axis because I instantly got dizzy from it. "I caught a giant bat!"

She bolted toward me, arms flailing like off-balanced propellers, pole still in one hand, dragging the giant, by-anyone's-standard, bat behind her like a kite. "Get it away!" she screamed as she swooned in on me, covering her head with her free arm, and tucked her head into my chest. Still connected to the pole she was holding; the bat circled our heads like it was teasing a landing on one of us. One of her hands wrapped around my waist, her fingers curled around the small of my back and she dug her nails deep into my skin.

It didn't *hurt* and I easily breathed right through it.

Who was I kidding? She had malignant Edward Scissorhands and I was close to tears! Desperate to stop her from slicing right through me, I took the pole from her, pleading, "You have to cut the line loose!" I tried to sound cool, but it was breathtaking in a knee-shaking sort of way how huge that thing encircling our heads was—the size of an eagle really!

"I don't have scissors!" she called from my armpit.

Sure, you do. Attached to your fingers!

"Just chuck your pointy shoe at it!" I wailed, fighting back my own tears of pain.

"Not funny." She covered her head even more with her arm and continued to cower into me, pressing her body into mine.

That part wasn't really that bad.

Maybe I like bats?

I put the line up to my mouth, trapping it in my back teeth, and gnawed on it until it snapped loose. The bat fluttered ungraciously away. We were left standing *way* too close for a casual encounter.

Even through my T-shirt, I could feel her frantic breath rush hot against my chest.

Yeah, I definitely like bats.

"He's gone," I whispered a little mournfully because it would only be seconds, and we'd have to act appropriately again. She didn't pull away. Instead, she looked up, hooking her eyes on mine, and they seemed to penetrate right through me like she had laser eye surgery. But not the kind that optically improved your vision. The kind that threatened me with actual lasers if I dared to move.

Not even a little extreme in my description. I was frozen—with fear of the lasers—totally afraid to move.

She didn't budge.

And I didn't budge.

Not even a toe.

Her body was still sandwiched against mine, and I could feel her heart racing from the bat attack.

My heartbeat competed with hers and was just as fast.

Mine wasn't racing from the bat.

I wasn't afraid of that bat.

I still really loved that bat. He was like my bro.

My heart was pounding because something was happening. Like a swelling, my heart was being pumped full of tiny seeds, tasked with the sole job of making my feelings about Atalie . . . *complicated.* Her arms were still wrapped around my waist, but she had loosened her stabby grip. It was comfortable holding her like this.

Actually, I enjoyed it.

When I looked back at her, I saw her with new eyes.

A beautiful, kind woman who had followed me to a *freaking* swamp. If this was a movie, violins would have chimed in, and butterflies would have risen from the ground as they fluttered around, framing our embrace.

It was a magical moment.

She *ruined* it by clearing her throat and stepping back. Rubbing her forehead like she was trying to hide her face behind her hand, she murmured, "Wow, that was crazy."

"Yeah," I muttered, wondering what had happened to our magical moment. My arms were still tingling from where her body had rested against mine. In a disappointed voice, I asked, "I wonder if he's going to come back."

Her eyes grew again, and before I could talk her out of it, she fled back up the riverbank, calling behind her, "I'm not going to stay to find out!"

"Yeah, that would be horrible," I mumbled in partial agreement, as I picked up the poles, following her.

Not horrible.

Massive fan of bats.

Fourteen

Trey

It was dusk by the time we headed back, but we didn't get far before Atalie stopped on the trail. Hanging her head low, she panted out, "I have a super sensitive stomach and the lack of food is making me sick. I need to rest for a second."

"Ah, okay . . ." I looked around the trail, glossing over the piles of decayed leaves and overgrown brush until I spotted a large fallen log behind us. "Do you want to hang out here for a rest?"

She fanned her face, like she was fighting back waves of nausea. "Yeah, I need to give it a second and then I will be fine." We moved in unison toward the log and sat next to each other, looking straight ahead like two strangers waiting at the bus stop. "I'm confused," she started, in between her measured breaths. "When will you talk to Robert if he's off with his woman?"

"I'll talk to him tonight after she goes to bed," I answered assuredly. The weird thing was even though I came here to see Robert, it didn't bother me that he was busy. I found myself enjoying my time with Atalie.

She loudly swatted a mosquito that had landed on her arm. "I wish I still had my sweater to protect my arms from the bugs."

I gave her a smile I hoped showed my appreciation. "Just get through tonight, and we'll be back on the road in the morning."

"Are you telling me it's safe to start the countdown?"

"I'll tell you anything you want if it means you don't hate me after all this." I hadn't planned to say something like that. Something that came out sort of flirty, and I winced through narrowed eyes as I waited to see how she'd receive it.

Snickering behind a wrinkled nose grin, she asked, "What was that?"

I looked down at my shoe, feeling the aftershocks of how cheesy that was. "Clearly, I have no game."

She chewed on the side of her cheek, and it was the sort of fidget I didn't know how to read. It was nicer than a get-lost scowl but not exactly a friendly smile.

Contemplative at best.

Barely tolerant at worst.

I don't know why I all the sudden had this massive crush on Atalie. This was absurd! I literally just broke up with my girlfriend. Shouldn't I care about that? When I tried to think about how Tonya's voice sounded when she said my name—something I had always loved about her—I immediately road-blocked it. Instead rebounding to Atalie's sweet inflections.

Clearly this swamp encounter was making me crazy.

Maybe it was because Tonya and I had been doing the avoidance dance for months—both afraid to be the one to say the final words. I couldn't even remember why I had been afraid. Losing Tonya was nothing like I thought it would be. It felt nothing more or less than *right*—the way it was supposed to be.

"What are you thinking about?" Atalie asked after we had sat in silence for way too long.

"Truthfully, I was thinking about Tonya."

"Ah." Her empathy-infused voice was smooth when she cautiously asked, "Do you miss her?"

"Actually, that's what I was thinking about. It's weird, but I feel peaceful. It was right on so many levels."

"Maybe it hasn't hit you yet?"

I was surprised I was confiding in her. Normally, I had a hard time talking about this stuff. Obviously, if it took me months to end a broken relationship, my communication skills were lacking, but there was something about the softness etched in Atalie's voice, that seemed to peel my secrets right out of me. "It's been over for a long time and we both knew it, but we avoided talking about it. Almost like we were waiting until the feelings had all dissipated and we were able to part as friends. When I think about her, I only see how different we are, and I'm surprised we made it so long."

"Opposites attract."

"I guess. At first, anyway." The night shadows hit the planes of her face in a way that highlighted her natural beauty perfectly. Something about the stillness in the moment made me risk a personal question. "What was it like for you to lose the love of your life?"

Wrong thing to ask!

She was relaxed before, but I knew she immediately tensed up because I heard a light hiss when she inhaled.

Clearly, my joke about having no game was a foreshadowing. Who asks about a dead husband?

"You don't have to answer that," I spit out, wishing to take my stupidity back, but she was already speaking in a voice held up by a weakened breath, so I willingly shut my fat mouth and listened.

"It's like waking up every day hating the rules of time."

My gaze gravitated toward her, as I tried to understand. That explanation was not what I was expecting. "How do you mean?"

"Time only moves forward, but who says that's how it must be?" She flicked her slender hand toward me in a ladylike gesture of question. "I think most people would prefer it to have options." She slowly dragged her teeth along her bottom lip, and if I hadn't been so hyper-focused on how beautiful she looked, I would have missed her chin quiver ever so slightly.

Yep. Stupidest question I could have asked.

Now she was sad. I didn't want her to be sad.

This was when my deficient social skills went into overdrive, and I was left wondering what to do.

Should I pat her back and say there, there?*I think that only works with injured puppies.*

Um, leaning in for a hug would be a bit of a logistics hurdle with how we were sitting.

If she were a computer, I'd reboot her until she switched modes, but she didn't have a reboot button.

I didn't know what to do, so I did nothing.

And I did it well.

I didn't mind sitting here next to her.

She didn't run away, so that told me she didn't mind it either.

Or maybe I was only slightly better than being attacked by a swamp creature all alone?

I'd take it.

After a while, she turned her head farther toward me, and said, "I wouldn't be greedy. There's no way I'd want to live my life backward, but I would want one more day on repeat for eternity."

"Like a never-never land," I said in a hushed voice, not wanting to break her concentration.

She swapped her stoic expression for one daring more enchantment, piercing her eyes with a shimmer that radiated her inner beauty. "Exactly. When I allow myself to think about him, the strongest thought is I want to go back. Do you know what I mean?"

My brows flattened while I mused the comparison. "I don't think I've ever felt that way."

Turning her head more so she could fasten her gaze directly on mine, she paused briefly before saying, "Then I don't think Tonya was the love of your life. If she had been, it would hurt. You would want it back. They say you know it was right when it hurts."

A smooth wave of goosebumps proliferated up my arm nearest her, not stopping until they all seemed to pool in the center of my lips. Unavoidably, my lips parted as the stare she gave me cemented my body in place in a way I'd never felt before.

I couldn't move.

I didn't want to.

I just nodded.

Her eyes seemed to carve into mine, etching their own place that left a burn lingering deep into my core. They raged a war in my brain, begging me to surrender to her powers.

I totally wasn't letting my imagination run wild.

Unfortunately, she had the *worst* timing for ruining moments and her eyes flicked back toward the trail. "We should go back. It's super dark now."

Just like that, I knew exactly what she had meant. I wanted a pause button with a hint of rewind. I, too, hated the rules of time.

Fifteen

Atalie

I never had the feeling I wanted to be in two places at once. Part of my brain was flashing red alarms, warning me to stay away from Trey. The other part of my mind was starved for that level of human connection, yearning to stay near him longer. But I wasn't stupid. He was only hanging out with me because I was helping him. He was a billionaire and billionaires weren't interested in their housekeepers. In addition, he was obviously uncommitted because he strung his last girlfriend along for *twenty years* without ever marrying her. I would never be interested in that sort of arrangement, so for all these reasons, I stayed guarded.

Pushing all my yearning curiosity aside, I stood, knowing it was time to go back to the village. We were immersed in the night and eerily quiet would be the nicest way I could describe the vibe I was getting. Not taking chances on the wild and deadly out here, I grasped Trey's wrist like a defiant child who needed to be dragged back out of a busy intersection. I flashed him a toothy grin and reminded him, "Remember you volunteered to be sacrificed first."

He started to carefully step forward, leading us back. Even though he looked relaxed, my trepidation was building to maximum levels because it was hard to see even a few feet in front of us. Each step produced a new sound: a cracking of a stick or crunching of leaves that told us it was safe to proceed. We'd stayed out way too late, and my heart protested wildly in my chest, screaming a reality check at how reckless I had been to be out here. I took shallow steps, but I made the mistake of not lifting my foot high enough as I scooted to safety and then—wham! *It happened.*

My foot hooked a vine, sending me face-first into the mud!

My immediate danger was over, but my brain didn't know. It propelled me into a state of immense panic which bled into my bones. I let out the most scared-for-my-life horror-filled scream I could muster as I desperately tried to run but was held back by my foot still entangled in the vine.

Trey dropped to a knee, silencing my scream with the palm of his hand. "Quiet, or they'll hunt you because you sound like a mad animal," he warned, but added in a sympathetic tone, "You're fine. It's only a root."

I heard his words, but my heart was off to the racetrack, and scared tears hooded my eyes. In a shaken voice, I begged, "Please, get me out of this!"

I trembled through the several times it took Trey to yank on the vine until it finally broke and then he quickly unraveled the last of it from my foot. I wasn't thinking. I was out of my mind when I flew free of the vine toward him, landing on the front of his chest, and blurted out, "Oh, I love you!"

I froze, staring forward at the extremely firm chest I was clenching.

Oh man! Totally not what I wanted to say!

The silence was pulsating, so I tried to take it back. "I mean, I l-love you like a brother . . ."

Shut up! You're making it worse. A brother?

But I didn't shut up. I started to stutter, "Or, I-I a-appreciate you . . . or, shoot."

What are you saying, you blubbering moron?

Before it got worse, I backed off his chest, giving it a good natured thank-you pat. I was so insanely glad it was dark, but I still wished I had some invisible powers to turn on and I murmured, "I'm shutting up now." Keeping my chin tucked to avoid the bewilderment in his eyes, I latched back on to his wrist and waited for him to propel me forward.

I think he was equally stunned because he didn't try to speak as we continued our path. Thankfully, he did break the so-thick-it-was-stale silence as we rounded the final bend leading up to my hut. "Robert was telling me this area has flash flooding most days. If you get up early and the cottage is surrounded by water, you might want to wait until it recedes to ensure there isn't anything hiding in it."

Staring forward at my hut, I couldn't dare make eye contact with him. "You have such a way with words, don't you?"

His lips curled up in the corner when he stole a sideways look at me. "It was just a warning because I don't want anything to happen to you."

"I suppose it's too much to ask for a mint on my pillow." I stopped on my heel. At this point, I was extremely relieved to know all I had left to do was go in there to sleep. In the morning, I'd wake up and we could get out of here. When I turned to him, I was still too ashamed to look him in the eyes. "Good luck on your midnight negotiations."

"Thanks." Before he had a chance to say anything else, I quickly walked down the path to my cabin like I couldn't get away fast enough and disappeared through the front door, desperate to sleep this shame away.

Sleep never came. Instead, I shed tears.

I wept because I was embarrassed by how I had acted in front of my boss—the person I depended on for a livelihood. I cried because I was scared for my safety, and it was irresponsible for me to come here when I had a son back home who I missed terribly. I never asked for this life. The life of a widow, raising a son by herself. But I didn't complain because I had experienced an amazing love—married to my best friend. I wouldn't change anything about it. Well, except for the time thing, but there was nothing I could do about that.

These tears were rooted deep.

I cried because of the new feelings taking hold of my heart. Feelings I would never willingly allow myself to feel for someone other than my husband. I wasn't sure how it happened, but Trey had me thinking about *him*. When I thought about Trey, he made me want to move on . . .

Then I'm wrecked.

I promised forever—and to me—there was only one definition of the word.

Continuous.

Unfaltering.

I always imagined a love that continued after death.

I had planned on growing old with my husband, holding hands as we withered in old age, dying in the other's arms to only be reunited in the afterlife.

Promises didn't change because your reality didn't fulfill your expectations.

Thinking about what Trey did to my heart was like trying to win a battle, but the only weapon you have is a full moon. It's beautiful—sometimes hauntingly so—but what damage can it take without throwing the entire world off balance, if not destroying it. It was a battle that was not meant to be won.

I never asked for any of this.

Sixteen

Trey

"How did it go last night?" Atalie asked as soon as she opened the front door and found me on the step, waiting for her. Her face was still masked in mud. I struggled to hold back a smile because her lack of vanity was endearing and even with war paint, she looked beautiful to me.

"Everything went according to plan." Lowering my voice, I added, "I don't want to talk about it until we are out of here, though."

"Oh, okay." She took the descending steps away from the hut, watching the ground as she walked.

I walked closer to her, stumbling over my own foot, resembling a clumsy toddler who didn't know how to work his legs. Atalie's presence was having an effect on me I couldn't brush off. I had been excited to see her this morning but this somber expression she gave me had my heart constricting in a way which left me breathless. Out of ideas for words, I held up the oars Robert had given me. "I came prepared this time with two sets."

"That's good." Her voice seemed tired, and she hardly looked at me. "Is everything settled for us to leave?"

"Yeah," I said enthusiastically, expecting to hear her rejoice. Yet, she only offered me a weary smile as she headed down the worn path back to the river. Though she stayed right on my heel, she didn't hook her arm onto mine.

She had to be upset with me.

Okay, I know she was upset with me for bringing her here, but something beyond that.

"Is everything okay?" I eventually asked, letting my eyes linger on her face, searching for clues to what she was thinking. "I mean, aside from all of the extraordinarily life-threatening stuff I've put you through?"

Her lip didn't even twitch at my joke.

I blurted out the first thing that came to mind, "Is this about the lawyer thing?"

She pinned a perplexed indention between her brows. "What?"

"Do you remember how you asked for my lawyers' info?"

She shook her head but didn't seal her lips as she replied, "No. I wasn't thinking about that." She lowered her head down again. Now we were near the river's edge, and she caught her reflection in the water and let out an amused gasp. "Why didn't you tell me I looked like Chewbacca?"

Her words came out like a lightning bolt that shot through my ear and did a loopy loop around my brain, landing somewhere in the vicinity of my heart, making it pound harder. *A woman who speaks* Star Wars *is a woman after my heart! It was like poetry.* "Ah, Chewbacca is hairy, not dirty," I teased.

"I knew that. Well, I mean, I should know that. Josiah is pretty good at ensuring I'm up on my *Star Wars*. I was mostly referencing the brown color." She knelt, lapped the water in the palm of her hand, and scrubbed her face, venting, "Everyone talks about how bad technology is for our mental health, but nobody mentions how harmful a lack of it can be." She used her bare arm to swipe away the excess water dripping from her chin but was unsuccessful. I didn't have anything close to a towel, so I offered the sleeve of my favorite worn hoodie and she willingly leaned forward and dried her face with it. I had expected to see her gaze soften, but she held her stiff expression, her eyes fleeing back to the water.

She wouldn't even look at me.

Could I blame her, though? I dragged her out here. In my defense, I had no idea it would be this bad. But lucky for us both, we only had one boat ride upriver before we'd reunite with our guide, and that should cheer her up.

I walked over to the boat I had stored upside down on a large rock and pulled it to the water. Clenching the back ridge to hold it steady, I looked over at her, saying, "You can climb in first." She crossed before me, stepping into the boat without glancing back. I handed her the extra set of paddles before I found my way into the boat, sitting in front of her. Taking a minute to balance the weight between the two of us, I then set my paddles and started to row, calling out, "After while crocodiles." She followed my lead in rowing but didn't crack a sound at my joke. I caved in the silence. "Atalie." My voice came out raspy like it does when I'm nervous, so I cleared my throat. "I'm sorry if this was too much for you. I didn't know it would be this bad."

Since I couldn't see her face, I had to rely on the pacing of her breath to know how she was feeling. I didn't notice any growling or hissing, so I figured that was good.

"It has been too much," she finally said.

Part of my heart was heavy, knowing how hard this had been for her, but the other part of my heart told me it was going to work out. Now I needed to make sure she didn't hate me. "For what it's worth, thank you."

"I hope it paid off."

"It did. It may seem extreme to you to go through all of this, but Robert was the only person I could trust, and I knew unless I talked to him in person, he wouldn't really understand how strongly I felt about that. As you can probably tell, I'm not the best with this stuff. But it worked out, and Robert's going to fly out at the end of the month. He's all the way on board with taking over my software division."

"Wait," she interrupted me. "What about his fiancée?"

"She'll come too. That's why they must wait. I'll get everything set up for them and they will run away in the middle of the night so they can elope."

She sucked in a loud breath. "Are you kidding?"

"No," I tried to keep my tone respectful. "This is a tribe who still does a lot of arranged marriages and having your daughter marry a foreigner is not something they would ever approve of."

"But not being able to see your family member get married is better?"

"In their eyes, it allows them to be together."

"I had no idea it was like that." Her voice was filled with astonishment when she went on, "I can't believe she is willing to lose her entire family for a chance to be in love. I couldn't imagine being that brave."

"Sure, you can. If you think about it, you risked your life to help me this weekend and you barely know me."

Why, like seriously WHY? Why did I remind her she's risking her life again? I gritted my teeth while I screamed at myself. She was mute. Clearly, I had stuck my foot in my mouth again. And not a little like the toe. It was way up to my knee in there and I wanted to smack myself. She had finally started to talk again, and I ruined it. Surprisingly, she spoke again but in a dreamy tone, "It's a beautiful love story, isn't it?"

"Yeah," I agreed, thankful I hadn't made her shut down again. "I hope it works out for them and they find a way to stay connected to her family, so it doesn't end in tragedy."

Without wasting a breath, she added, "From my experience, most beautiful love stories do."

Seventeen

Trey

Astonishingly, Atalie didn't resign the moment we got on US soil. She did, however, make sure to get my lawyers' info and eagerly accepted a week off. It was oddly quiet in the house, and every time I set down to get some work done, I found myself missing seeing her crazy headbands and old-lady sneakers running past my office. Topped with the immense guilt I had for dragging her through last weekend, I couldn't get her out of my brain.

Okay, I admit it.

It wasn't so much the guilt as it was this new crush I had.

I just wanted to see her.

Although it was her week off, I texted her.

Me: *Do you think you can swing by the house for a minute? I have something I need to show you.*

Atalie: *Is everything okay?*

Me: *I hope so. If you're busy it can wait, but I hope you don't.*

Atalie: *Be over in thirty.*

Me: *Bring Josiah.*

Atalie: *Okay.*

It was exactly thirty minutes later, and I heard chatter coming from the entryway. They were the same voices I had gotten used to hearing over the last few weeks, so it shouldn't have felt any different, but it did. Nervous energy budded in my extremities. I had the urge to fidget, pace, or do anything to be busy. Unable to wait for them to get to my office, I met them halfway down the hall—all my enthusiasm displayed in the awkward curl of my lips as if my grin alone was responsible for keeping a secret only I had privilege too.

"What's the surprise?" Atalie's eyes flickered with interest, locking on mine when she saw me. The way she looked at me said it was all going to be worth it.

"Well, it's a two-part surprise. One part is for you"—I shifted my gaze to meet Josiah's— "and the second part is for you."

"Me?" Josiah's head sprang back like it was a trigger that set off the sparkle in his eyes. "What did you get me?"

"Remember, that's the second surprise, and we need to take a short trip to get there." I latched my eyes back on Atalie's, feeling a cocktail of emotions—excited to see her, relieved I didn't have to miss her anymore, more excited to see her get surprised, overwhelmed by my nerves which seemed to show up at the most inconvenient times and something else. Something I couldn't define, but it made me bite down on my lip—hard. I blurted out, "Let's take your car."

"Ha ha." Atalie rolled her eyes, but not in the exaggerated way a teenager would. It was cute way and seemed flirtatious. "You know I don't have a car."

"Now you do." I held up my hand, letting a key fob hang down. It was a simple action, but somehow my whole heart felt on display. It immediately caught Atalie's eye, and I adored the way her jaw fell. Her animation showed me everything she was feeling. "I couldn't get purple," I managed to tease as I struggled to get words out because my chest felt like someone had rammed a truck into it. I wasn't prepared to feel so terrified of rejection, and I was stuttering, "I . . . I hope it's okay that I got red."

"What . . ." Her eyes clung to mine like she was afraid to look directly at the fob, but the exclamation on her lips hinted she understood exactly what it was without looking.

I pushed the key fob forward, but she still didn't take it. I grabbed her hand—prayed she didn't notice how suddenly clammy my hand felt—and placed the fob centered in her palm, closing her fingers around it so it wouldn't fall out. "It's a gift."

"Why would you get me a car?" Her voice was a little stronger now, but it still wasn't close to her typical inflections.

Instead of answering her question—talking was not working because my chest was so tight, I'd sound like Mickey Mouse if I tried—I motioned to the garage door on the other end of the hall, and somehow managed to say, "Go check it out."

She and Josiah both scurried down the hall and pushed through the door at the same time, reminiscent of excited kids on Christmas. "Tell me that's not a Mercedes logo." The excitement was escalating in her voice, and I couldn't take my eyes off her.

"I got you the SUV because I thought it would be nice and roomy for you and Josiah."

She looked at the car, before her eyes returned to me. Then she swept her eyes back to the car before raising both brows and fixing her eyes steady on me. "You're serious?"

"Of course, I'm serious." *Okay, I did hear a minor squeak in my voice that time. New plan. Deep breath and focus on lowering my tone.*

"Why would you get me a car?"

I raised one shoulder, feeling it should be obvious and maybe I was still scared to talk, but she kept staring at me like she was expecting me to talk, so I forced out, "We talked about it, remember?"

"As a joke." Her eyes took another pass at the car, glittering over it. "This is way too much of a gift."

"It's a minor work benefit." I couldn't handle talking anymore. As much as I loved being a boss who could spoil his staff, *this* wasn't really about that.

This was about Atalie.

I was selfish in that I had wanted a reason to see her on her week off, and I wanted her to *like* me. Even more, I loved the softness etched in the stolen glances she gave me in between the exploratory looks she gave her car. I could have bottled that moment if it had been an option. But there was still another huge part of the surprise, so I clapped my hands once and ushered them toward the car, opening the driver's side car door for her. "You still have another surprise, and you get to drive."

"This is crazy," she said, but she didn't need more convincing before hopping into the driver's seat. I ran around to shotgun while Josiah jumped in the back. "Okay." She looked at me, her eyes filled with wonder. "Where am I going?"

"I typed the address in the GPS."

"Another secret."

"It's easier to show you than to explain it."

She gave me a sassy quirt of an eyebrow. "And you promise it's not a swamp thing?"

I picked up on her playfulness. "It's not a swamp or a shredder."

Her lips caved beautifully, pinning the most perfect smile in place, brightening her face like an ambient light that produced the perfect canvas for every emotion on the spectrum of joy. Catching me completely off guard, I was captivated by her and spent the next nine minutes trying not to stare.

"It looks like some sort of a school," Atalie thought out loud when she pulled into the long private drive a few minutes later. She glanced at me briefly, "Is this it? Should I park?"

"Right up here." I motioned to the visitor parking spots. "They're expecting us."

"I'm so confused right now," Atalie said as she hopped out of the car. "I seriously thought we were going to have lunch."

I chuckled, totally feeling food would have been a good surprise too. "Are you hungry?" I waited on the sidewalk for them to join me. "We can grab something when we're done."

"I was hungry. Now I'm excited and you know how my sensitive stomach gets." Atalie flashed me a warning look and patted her middle.

"It won't take that long." I put my hand on her lower back, guiding her forward up the front steps, past the colonnade façade. Looking back at Josiah, who was still lagging, dragging his feet I called to him, "Come on, Josiah. This is all about you."

He gave me a coy smile, hinting he was being shy of me. I realized although, I had seen him almost every day, I hadn't ever gone out of my way to engage with him before. I understood how this might feel odd to him. I slowed my steps, synchronizing with his. "Have you figured it out yet?"

"It's a private school. It said so on the sign." His voice was unimpressed, like I would expect any kid his age to think about school.

"It is," I agreed as we pushed through the heavy doors. "I went to school here, and it's one of the best private schools in the country. I can't wait for you to see it." My voice trailed off at the end because I saw my friend, Tony, waiting for us outside of his office door. "Good morning, Tony." I reached out, shaking his hand, and then put a hand on Josiah's shoulder. "This is the young man I was telling you about. His name is Josiah. He's exceptionally bright and excited to see your school today."

"Nice to meet you, Josiah." Tony reached out to shake Josiah's hand. Josiah received his hand but eyed Tony suspiciously, like he wasn't sure what planet he was from. I should have probably prepped Josiah a little more about why we were here. Tony turned to Atalie with his hand still extended. "I'm Tony Bran, the Headmaster here. Nice to me you—"

"That's Atalie. She's my . . ." I should have let her introduce herself, but I felt like since I was the shared link, I had to make the connection, but I got stuck. I didn't want to say maid because that sounded so demeaning. Never thought about it before, but she needed a better title. She definitely was so much more than a maid. "She's my, ah . . . She's my Atalie." I went stone-faced when I heard how that sounded, and the heat in my face flushed all the way to my ears.

Atalie took Tony's hand. "I'm Josiah's mother, Atalie. I work for Trey. Nice to meet you, Mr. Bran."

"And you as well." After shaking Atalie's hand, Tony looked back to Josiah. "Would you like to see my school?"

Josiah's eyes floated to his mom, who grinned back at him. When Josiah looked back to Tony, he shrugged. "I guess."

Tony led the way, talking directly to Josiah. "Our school has two main concerns. One, futurism is at the head of everything we teach. Our programs teach information valuable today and in years to come. However, we can't just teach futurism, unless we understand our past. We pride ourselves on having ample literature studies to assist our history programs and we have one of the most impressive libraries, housing both physical and digital collections. We also have extensive creative time to round everything out."

He stopped in front of a room that was filled with students about Josiah's age but none of the students were sitting at a desk. They were spread out around the room, working at different stations on everything from building bridges out of wooden popsicle sticks, constructing robots, painting rocks and even a random student standing on his head against the wall. "This is our creativity lab," Mr. Bran went on. "Every student has equal lab time to seat time daily to do self-directed projects. We have found it enticing to our students to be able to tell them, first we are going to learn about something, and then we are going to go *do* it."

Josiah's eyes fluttered around the room, and I could see a smile start to bud behind his tight lips.

"How much time did you say they spend in lab?" Atalie asked while her eyes also glided around the room.

"It works out to be fifty-fifty," Mr. Bran replied, keeping her eye contact. "It sounds like a lot, but we have found test scores actually improve with less seat time when that seat time is swapped out for hands-on activities."

"It makes sense," I said. "I like being able to move around when I work. I would have the hardest time sitting all day."

"Right." Mr. Bran nodded in agreement. "As stewards of your child's education, we put ourselves in their shoes with every decision we make. Our evaluations are unique in that most of the time teacher evaluations are an assessment of the teacher's lectures and test scores. I, and the rest of my department heads, participate in the programs like a student would in order to fulfill our assessments. So, I will—several times a year—come in here to participate as a student would and I get to see it through their eyes. We have found it opens the door of communication between the student and the administrators when we work as peers. It's a forward model of education with the best part being when the students enter high school, we swap out lab time for internships. They spend half of their time in the community applying what they have learned, while also researching potential interests." His eyes rested on Josiah's when he asked, "What do you think? Would you like to go to school here?"

Josiah's eyes rounded out like he wasn't sure what was going on, but before he could respond, Mr. Bran went on, "We have a three-year waiting list, and once your name comes up on the list, you are required to sit for an entrance exam which tests your critical thinking skills but . . ." He paused, looked over to me, before returning his focus to Josiah and winked. "We worked it out, and we will have a seat for you this fall if you choose to attend."

Josiah's gaze wavered between his mom and Mr. Bran, but he didn't utter a sound. Atalie spoke up, "It's fine to not decide right now, Bud. We will discuss it later, okay?" Josiah didn't answer, he instead looked back into the lab room, an evident interest growing in the sparks of his eyes.

The bell rang, and all the students busied themselves with stowing away their materials, then headed down the hall to go outside. "We also have four outside recesses a day," Mr. Bran explained as he looked at Josiah. "One between each period to give them plenty of fresh air." Then he added, "Would you like to join them in their recess today? I can introduce you to my nephew who would love to show you the playground."

Josiah's eyes floated up to Atalie's like he still wasn't sure what was going on, but Atalie didn't waste any time ushering him toward the mad rush of students outside the door. "Go outside. Have fun." Her lips pulled into a smile as she watched him leave with Mr. Bran.

I was so charged with curiosity; I couldn't wait any longer to know what Atalie was thinking. "What do you think?" I asked, "Isn't it perfect for him?" She interlaced her fingers in front of her while keeping her head down, not meeting my enthusiasm. It was apparent she was purposely averting my gaze. My stomach immediately dropped, and I felt ill. *I somehow messed up.* I leaned forward. "What's wrong? You don't like it?"

"I can't believe you would bring him here without talking to me about it first." Her voice was soft and dithering. "Now he will have this expectation of building robots all day. There is no way I can afford something like this."

"Oh." Relief flooded my veins when I realized I had only messed up the communication part of the surprise. I tacked on quickly, "I forgot to tell you. *That* was the surprise. I'm paying for it."

Her lips pinched together, and she shook her head adamantly. "No, you are not. It's way too much."

"No, really." I leaned forward, still trying to see her expression, but she tucked her chin down. I had no idea if I was making her uncomfortable or if she hated the school so I added casually, trying to make it sound like no big deal, "I donate so much money to this school every year that I should actually own a few of these scholarship students." I chuckled at my joke, but her lips didn't bend. I added in a softer tone. "I do really want to do this for him."

"Why?" She looked up now, smacking her eyes with mine in a way that felt a little accusatory.

I nervously shuffled my feet and coddled out, "What do you mean, why?"

"I mean, why all the gifts?" She looked around the room like she was looking for the catch but when there wasn't anything, she set her eyes back on me. "I don't understand what this is about. It's one thing to let me use your car, but Josiah is my son. I don't know why you would bring him into this."

I shrugged, not really understanding why her tone would be harsh when I expected her to be beaming with excitement. This was totally backfiring. All I was trying to do was make her like me. Realizing I took it too far, I played down my gestures. "Lots of companies give educational benefits. I thought it would be nice because he seems bored sitting at my house all day."

Her lips parted but no words came out. Her tongue hovered her bottom lip before she closed her mouth back up, sealing her lips. She was clearly not going to say anything. I was trying to fix my mistake of taking her to the swamp, but now I was scared I had made things even worse with her. My nervous chatter button turned on, and my words just tumbled out, "Do you know why I moved back to New York?" I didn't let her answer, and went on, "I had issues—a lot of issues—with staff. Everything from stealing, to leaking trade secrets, to general disrespect. I was over it. I needed to be with people I trusted. It left me disabled in my ability to even hire anyone. That's the honest reason why my mom was the one who hired you. I had no confidence in my ability to read people. Lucky for me, she found you, but I messed up . . ." I paused, took a breath, and I mentally applied a filter to my words before I said something that was too much. "I shouldn't have asked you to go to Indonesia with me. I was manic and I can't believe I pushed you into it."

"It worked out—" She tried to brush my comment away, but I cut her off.

"Barely." I put my hand on her shoulder, squaring my face with hers. "I fully expected you to quit the moment we got home, and you had every right to because I was insane. You didn't quit." I let my gaze wander to the side, trying to be intentional with each word. "Then I saw you were exactly the person I needed. Your loyalty is worth everything to me, and I don't care if you're my maid, assistant or whatever you decide to do in my company. I want you to stay. I'm happy to do whatever it takes to show my appreciation because if there is one thing I have learned, it's that the most important thing anyone can ever give you is their loyalty."

In my head, my grandiose speech won her over. However, when she did finally manage to pull her eyes back to meet mine, I could still see a layer of skepticism revealing, although she had earned my trust, I still had a way to go in earning hers'. Blame it on the swamp thing—possibly—I was okay with that because I was willing to be patient. "Sooo," I drug out the word to make it a full sentence. "What are you thinking?"

"I'm thinking," she started, letting her words trickle out slowly. "It's very generous of you. I just hope you are not messing with my son because I will kill you if I find out you are."

I sputtered out a laugh, but when she didn't even smile, I held up a finger like I understood her point. "Right. Your pointy shoe."

That finally earned me the smile I was craving, and as soon as I saw it, my heart swelled. I hadn't realized how tense this interaction was for me, but

I felt my shoulders relax now. “Should we check on Josiah or do you want me to show you how to steal chocolate milk from the kitchen?”

“I may be loyal”—Her face held an air of teasing again— “But I will not be your accomplice in crime.”

“It was a test,” I retorted, “that you clearly passed.” My smile consumed my face as I started to walk forward, saying, “Let’s go get Josiah and grab some lunch.” Then I tacked on, “That I will *pay* for.”

Eighteen

Atalie

After dropping Trey back off at his house, I drove home in silence. Josiah was in the back seat, but he appeared lost in his own world as he gazed out the window. I'm sure the school tour had him thinking about all kinds of things. I wasn't going to pry. It was a lot to process. He'd tell me when he was ready.

I—on the other hand—felt like my heart had been bowled over by a planet-sized ball with spikes. I was so heart sick it should not have been legal for me to drive in this state.

I never saw Trey coming.

He was never in my plan, and even though I had been wrestling with this weird attraction to him for a while, it wasn't anything I couldn't restrain. There was no way I could keep these feelings in my heart contained after a day like today.

There was also no way to explain what Trey did today—for me *and Josiah*—without thinking there was something hidden in his intentions. No boss would be that thoughtful. Even if they were rich, they'd cut a check for a bonus and call it good.

This wasn't about a job anymore.

I chewed on the end of my thumbnail as I pulled into my driveway and put *my car—the car Trey had just given me*—into park. This would have been enough, but he didn't stop there.

He included Josiah.

I'm done.

Feelings for Trey were unleashed.

Nineteen

Trey

Atalie finished the rest of the week off, but she did text me several photos of her driving her new wheels. She was obviously enjoying it, which made me happy I could do that for her. I stayed busy making arrangements to install Robert as vice president of my company. That required tying up a lot of loose ends and as part of one of them, I called Evan.

"Sup?" he answered.

"Did you get my email about my needing another computer for Robert?"

"I did, but it's my new normal to take two days to read your emails, and I give myself another week to reflect on your requests before I require myself to respond. Your expectation of instant gratification is no longer compatible with my life goals."

"You overslept?"

"Nah, I didn't want to work."

"Nice life."

"I don't mind it. Actually, I was fired from my first job for bringing my infamous we-should-all-quit vibe to work. I've always been an overachiever in slacking, and I wouldn't want to quit now."

"Does your busy schedule allow you to squeeze in your only client?" I smarted back.

He let out a sigh like he was being deeply inconvenienced. "I'm obviously booked today, but I should be able to drop it off tomorrow."

"Tomorrow is perfect."

His voice rolled out in a low chuckle like he was about to cut into a giant piece of perfectly cook meat. "Then you can introduce me to your new maid."

My head jolted like I needed to check my hearing. "My what?"

"Didn't you say you got a new maid?"

My chest constricted when I understood he was asking me about Atalie. Suddenly, I felt protective of her. "Yeah . . . I did, but you can't . . . meet her."

"Just because you have had a girlfriend forever doesn't mean you can't empathize with us eternally single people."

"I don't have a girlfriend anymore," I said, realizing how weird that felt to say out loud. It was totally bizarre I was more affected by him asking about Atalie.

"What?"

"Yeah, we broke up." Answering this question felt annoying to me. It was a waste of my time to even talk about Tonya.

"I don't blame her because she was too good for you anyway."

"Thanks. I know who to call when I need a confidence boost."

"No prob."

"So, is that why you don't want me to meet your maid?"

"I don't . . . w-what?" Stuttering like a school kid who had been called out for sleeping in class, I wondered if he could tell I had feelings for Atalie. Not that there was anything wrong with them, but she didn't know about them. I sure didn't want her to find out through stupid Evan. I played cool. "That doesn't make sense."

"I mean, if you want it to make sense . . . It could. It could be a really cute Hallmark movie."

"Shut up."

"I'll see you tomorrow."

I ended my call, feeling like I had almost been caught doing something illegal and I was about to put my phone down, but a new text message flashed on my screen.

Tonya: *I'm in town, getting the last of the things from my apartment. I found some sentimental things of yours you might want back—like your high school chess club T-shirt and your autographed Yoda baby doll.*

Me: *It's not a doll. It's a collector's item so get that straight.*

Tonya: *Right. Well anyway, would you like to meet for lunch, and I can give you these things?*

Me: *Sure. Does noon work? I can meet you at the Thai restaurant around the corner from your place.*

Tonya: *Sure. See you.*

Me: *Confirmed.*

Setting my phone down on my desk, I thought about how odd it was that I hadn't missed Tonya. Sure, some songs had come on the radio and tossed a memory of her back in my mind, but I wasn't pining for her. I did have a box of her stuff I had cleaned out, and thought we might as well get together to do the tradeoff.

One of the perks about working from home was I worked in a T-shirt and jeans on most days, but today I was still in my sweatpants. I didn't want her to think I had gone over the deep end and stopped showering since we'd broken up, so I headed upstairs to clean up. After a quick shower, shave, and clothes that didn't look slept in, I stood in the mirror, wrestling with some stubborn hair gel when I felt someone looking at me.

Atalie was in the doorway, holding a stack of fresh towels. It was the first time I had seen her since I'd surprised her. Even though I had thought about her every other second of every day, I tried to play it cool. She held her hand up in a soft nonmoving wave.

I mimicked her wave while still holding the bottle. Instead of looking smooth, I came out looking like I was auditioning for a commercial to sell hair gel. I fumbled for a second, setting the gel on the counter. "I didn't hear you arrive."

"We were quiet, and I saw your office was empty, so I cleaned it." She held up the towels. "And I got a load of towels washed already."

"Thanks." I took them from her and turned to put them in the linen closet. "How was your time off?"

"I can proudly say we hit up almost every drive-through within a twenty-mile radius. And . . ." She paused, her lashes lowered, hooding her eyes before continuing in a soft voice, "I thought about how I acted at the school, and I felt bad. I was confused but I wanted you to know I do appreciate the offer of sending Josiah to school." She raised her eyes back to mine. "I can't ever repay you but thank you. If the offer still stands, he would love to go to school there."

Suddenly my palms felt tacky, even though I had just gotten out of the shower. "Of course, the offer stands and no need to repay, and you're welcome," I tried to echo her soft tone, but I started to get the vibe that the expression she had for me held *more* than a thank you.

Or maybe I was just hoping it was.

Because that would be neat.

Her eyes drifted to the top of my head. "Are you gelling your hair?"

"Ah, yeah, I don't normally, but I've been too busy to get a haircut. I had a weird spikey thing going on in the front. I thought it might help tame it." Her body being so close to me had this disabling power and I was unable to think of anything normal to say. Not wanting her to leave, I struggled to converse more, and felt stupid words tumble out, "What do you think about hair gel?"

Her forehead puckered, but her eyes stayed on the bottle. "Are you asking for my opinion on your hair?"

"Yeah," I deadpanned, unsure where I was going with the conversation, but if it kept Atalie near me, I was going to try it out.

"It's fine."

Words. Use words, Trey.

I managed a single, "But . . ."

"It's not a but." She stepped farther into the bathroom, joining me in looking into the mirror at my reflection. "*However,* most people have one feature of their face that is their best feature, and you should want to highlight that, right?"

My curiosity was piqued as to why she had so much to say about hair gel, and I replied with a simple, "Right."

"If a woman has nice eyes but a big nose, she should apply her makeup in a way that draws attention to her eyes, while at the same time minimizes the focus on her nose."

I stared down my nose at my reflection. "Is this your passive-aggressive way of telling me I have a big nose?"

"No. I'm saying when you spike your hair up, it draws attention to your hair, and it's okay." She offered a lazy one-shoulder shrug. "It does take away the focus from your best feature, though."

I blinked, feeling flattered. "So, that's your passive-aggressive way to say I have nice eyes?"

Shaking her head the slightest bit, her eyes dropped to my mouth, lingering there. "From a female perspective, your best feature is your lips."

Torture.

Absolute agony watching her stare at my lips. I stood frozen—no, *incapacitated* by her lasers again—not really knowing what was happening or even what she was talking about anymore. I was mostly sure we weren't talking about hair gel at this point, but I had fast become a huge fan of it because it made her look at my lips like that.

We weren't talking anymore.

We stood cemented in our places, hanging onto the moment.

I did know one thing.

I was an expert in code.

And she told me I had nice lips.

That was *clearly* code for her wanting to kiss me.

Kissing wasn't rational, though, and clearly so unprofessional.

An HR nightmare waiting to implode.

Did I care about that? I pondered, as I felt a rush surge through my chest. I wasn't a total stranger to this feeling of lightness in my body. I had this feeling before, anticipation that steals the air in your lungs. It's akin to that sensation you get when you slowly hike up a wooden roller coaster. In the last lingering moment right before you crest, you pause and grip the rails, bracing for the fall. The ensuing rush of emotions—fear enmeshed with excitement, and the heated rush of living life to its fullest.

Yeah, all I cared about was the way she was looking at me.

She ruined the moment *again* by breaking the silence. "Did you have more meetings today?"

"Uh, no, I'm going to run out and meet Tonya for lunch." My words spewed out and I instantly regretted them, but I wasn't sure why.

No, I did know why!

She had just told me I had nice lips!

Keep your fat mouth shut and let her look at my lips!

"Oh." She lightly tugged on her earlobe as she shuffled her feet, taking a step closer to the door. "I'll let you get ready."

My tongue got knotted and I wanted to beg her to come back, but nothing worked and as quietly as she had appeared, she had left!

I was so stupid!

I stared at the space she had recently occupied but it was empty.

Raking my hands through my hair, I dug deep into the roots, yanking on the ends until it hurt. I wanted to scream like that kid in *Home Alone*. I was a complete and total moron. She *had* to know by now I had these feelings for her. There was no way I was ever smooth enough to conceal something like this. Why couldn't I be normal around her?

Be normal and ask her out.

That should be easy, but it wasn't.

I was going to have to come up with some sort of plan, or this was going to slay me. That I knew for sure, but not right now. I needed to clear my head and I let my eyes skirt around the room in desperate need of a distraction.

Conveniently my phone lit up with a text.

Tonya: *Sorry, Trey but I still have movers here. Can we meet tomorrow for breakfast before I fly out?*

Me: *Sure.*

Tonya: *I'll text you in the morning.*

Me: *Fine.*

Setting my phone down, I was disappointed it was only Tonya again. Not that I was expecting Atalie to text me when she was in my house. . . but it would have been nice. I took another look down the hall, confirming that Atalie was indeed gone.

Pull yourself together or she's going to think you're a freaking psycho.

Okay. I inhaled deep into my chest, releasing my humiliation, giving myself permission to move forward with my day. Since I didn't have to leave the house, the thought running through my head was I wanted to say hi to Josiah. I hadn't seen him since I took him to my school, and he seemed excited about it, but I wanted to check if he had any questions. I figured he'd be sitting in the kitchen doing his homework, and I headed down the back staircase to find him.

Actually, last night after Atalie had dropped me off, it struck me that Josiah and I had a lot in common, both losing our dads so young. I never had to move and leave my friends on top of everything else. I couldn't imagine how horrible that had been for him. "Hey, Josiah," I greeted him from where he sat hunched over at the table doodling on a sketch pad.

His eyes regarded mine, but his face remained indifferent. "Hi."

"I was wondering—" I stopped because uncertainty clouded his eyes. I figured he was shy, but I also reasoned he had to be bored out of his mind. Softening my voice, I continued, "Would you want to come to see my secret hideout?"

His eyes narrowed in skepticism. "What hideout?"

"Well, it's not really a secret, but it is a cool place to hang out. I thought you might want to explore a little." I waved him forward. "Come on. I'd love to show it to you."

"Ah, sure." He slid off his chair, the look of confusion lifting, and his brow rose with excitement while he followed me.

"So, just so we are clear," I explained as we walked. "This is a *man's* hangout."

"Okay, but where are we going?"

"I'm taking you to the coolest place in the house. It was the place my dad used to take me when I was little, and we did the manliest things—there's model ships to build, *Star Wars* movies to watch, unlimited root beer . . ."

"And where's that?"

"The attic."

TWENTY

Atalie

I ducked into the safety of the hall bathroom and gently shut the door, pressing my palm against my pounding heart. I had tried to clean, and it lasted only a few minutes. *I couldn't do it anymore.* Clueless about so much, but one thing was evident to me—I had fallen for Trey.

These feelings took root during our trip, but I swore to myself that once we got home, I would be able to ignore them, and go back to not thinking about him. That didn't happen. I thought taking some time off would help me to get some perspective, but he kept texting me random things, and not to mention the *gifts* he gave me. It was too much, and I couldn't fight it anymore, and *something went way wrong.* My heart opened to him.

It wasn't normal to *have Trey look at me like that!* It was obviously a farce because in his next breath he confessed he was getting ready for a *date* with Tonya. But he always went out with her. That wasn't new. But it was new. New again anyway.

Even if it wasn't Tonya—it would be someone else—and it would never be me because billionaires don't fall for women like me. I was okay with that—mostly. Or I would be okay, as long as I could get away from here.

Tears threatened to burn my already tender-from-crying eyes. *I can't feel like this.* I definitely didn't want Trey to find me like this—now or ever. I needed to look for a different place of employment because this wasn't working. I can't work for a guy I'm in love with while he dates someone else. Still, I needed a paycheck, so until I had a new offer, I would have to avoid him. There was no other way because I couldn't let these feelings grow anymore as they were already too much.

Just do my job and ignore him.

This wasn't hard.

This was titanium.

I took another moment to catch my breath, then ran my hands down the front of my skirt—to both smooth it out and wipe off the excess moisture from my hands. Before I lost my nerve, I headed back away from the parts of the house he usually dwelled in. I ended up on the far end of the hall, but I noticed the attic door was slightly ajar. I slowed my steps, careful to not disturb, but also felt a little investigative.

Figuring someone had left it opened by accident, I was going to shut it. However, faint sounds of laughter told me someone was up there. Not just someone—*Josiah!* My heart ticked up a notch as I didn't want him to get in trouble. I quietly stuck my head inside the door, peering up the little staircase, but I couldn't see him. More laughter. My anxiety went full throttle. *This was clearly my fault because I had failed to tell him the attic was off-limits, but he had ever wandered the house before*!

It was not like him to dig around in other people's stuff. I started to plow forward on a mission to grab him before he was found but halted fast on my heel when I heard Trey's voice. Trey wasn't mad. He was making a joke. "Where did Luke Skywalker get his bionic hand from?"

"Ah," Josiah's thinking interjection hummed. "A robot store?"

"No, a *second hand* store."

Josiah's laughter piped out, filling up the entire room in a way that also filled my heart. Trey's more amused chuckle rounded out the sound, sending waves of flurries that melted my heart right down to its core.

Why wouldn't my heart melt at the sound of that? My son bonding with the man I was falling for. It would be perfect if it wasn't for that elephant-sized caveat sending out alarms. *Trey would never fall for someone like me. He was dating Tonya again. This was clearly setting Josiah and me up for more heartbreak!*

Josiah had been through so much loss this last year, and the last thing he needed to do was get close to someone who'd he would have to forget about. I always believed things happen for a reason and the timing couldn't have been more profound. This only solidified my decision to quit.

"Okay, now look closely," Trey spoke up. "This looks like an illegal move, but it's called en passant. Basically, the pawn can capture an enemy pawn horizontally adjacent in one—" Backing out of the room, I shut out Trey's voice and slowly closed the door with a renewed sense of urgency deep in my gut, screaming I needed to find a new job. The sooner the better.Noise from down the hall jolted me. I took giant steps away from the attic door before almost running into Mrs. Michael.

"Atalie." A smile that showed she was equally as startled strained on her lips. "I was looking for you."

"Oh." I tried my best to sound breezy as I made sure my back was facing the attic. "What can I do for you?"

"I need a favor. It's my week to host my ladies book club." Her head tilted toward mine like she was ready to share a secret. "And I forgot all about it and I'm short on people. Would you be able to sub for this week?"

"Um, a book club, huh?" My eyes fell to the side as I weighed how much stuff I had to do. *I needed to start looking for another job today!*

She leaned in a step closer like it was an urgent request. "Oh, please. It sounds silly but I'm in a bit of a friendly competition with one of my friends to see who would have the best attendance on their week of hosting." Shaking her head like she knew it was ridiculous, she tacked on, "You'll have a lot of fun, and it won't take more than an hour or so."

I was beginning to see she wouldn't take no for an answer, and I also felt a little frantic about the fact Josiah was upstairs in the exact place she had warned me was private. Even though Trey was up there, I didn't know the logistics of how they came to be up there together. I didn't want to risk getting fired before I had another job. I hurried to make her happy so we could move away from this conversation and the door behind us. "I can come. Where did you say it was at?"

"I was trying to win the competition, so I planned my meeting on the beach."

I took a few steps away from the door, hoping she'd do the same. "Book club on the beach?"

She followed right in tow. "It's so relaxing and you'll enjoy the night out."

"Okay." I continued to move my feet away from the door, trying to act relaxed. "What time and what book?"

"Six, behind the pier and . . ." Her eyes skirted the room once before adding, "It doesn't really matter what book."

My brows knitted together. "Don't we all need to read the same book?"

"Well, yes, but it's such short notice, just pick one."

"Um, okay." Something didn't feel right about her vague plans, but I was focused on getting her away from the attic door in case Josiah would come bursting out. Without pause, I continued to lead her toward the steps, and cheerfully agreed, "That sounds great. I'll be there. Oh hey." I held up a finger like I was remembering something, but I was mostly trying to make up a diversion. "I, ah, was wondering . . . what's the last book you read?"

"Oh." Her brow flattened like she didn't see the reason for my question. "I wouldn't even remember. I don't do much reading."

Twenty-One

Trey

It was a mistake to come to the beach tonight with the high winds. We crossed the sand behind the pier where Mom said she walked earlier, and lucky for us the pier was empty. I suspected it had to do with the nearing storm. The only person I did see was a man walking his dog far out in the distance. "Where did you say you were?" I waited for her to give me some directions, but she was distracted, craning her neck as if she thought her earring would be walking toward her.

"Let's head back this way and start along the water," I planned out loud since she gave me nothing to go on. Before I could step, I startled by a voice from behind us.

"Hey, you guys."

I identified her voice before I turned around, but it didn't lighten my breath. If anything, I stiffened. Atalie was walking toward us with Josiah trailing behind her. "What are you doing here?" I called, wondering why she would pick tonight in this near storm to come out.

"I'm meeting your mom for her book club." Her eyes bounced to my mom, and I instantly got suspicious about what Mom was up to. I turned to her, shaking my head. "Since when do you have a book club?"

"Oh dear." Mom's hand flew to her chest. "Did I get my nights mixed up?" Looking over at me, she tacked on, "Tell me it's Wednesday, right?"

"No, Mother." I smiled, amused as I went on, "It's Tuesday and even if it was Wednesday, you still wouldn't have a book club."

"Oh hush." She playfully batted her hand at me, pushing the center of my chest. "It's a new thing I started." When she looked at Atalie, her face held an apology. "I'm deeply sorry, I have been so spacey lately. I forgot what night it was, but it's good we ran into you. I had asked Trey to help me find my earring. I think I lost it somewhere . . ." She scanned the beach a couple of times like she was scouting for the perfect place to sunbathe before pointing to the farthest point from where we stood. "Somewhere over there." Patting a long tote she had under her arm, she added, "I brought my metal detector." She made a deliberate look at Josiah as she pulled the wand out of the tote. "You know, young people are so much better with technology than us old people. Josiah, I bet, you'd be good at helping me work this thing. Why don't you come with me?" Her eyes smacked Atalie and she added, "I was also by the water. Can you and Trey go look way over there?"

A curious smile budded on Josiah's lips, and that's when I understood this was a trap—and little innocent Josiah had been in on it. My mom started walking away with a boisterous matchmakey smile on her face, and called back, "It'll just take a second for us to run over there."

Josiah was fast on her heels, with little snickers piping out of his mouth as the duo marched off together like they couldn't get away fast enough. A chuckle brewed in my chest because I was *stunned.* I figured Mom had been up to something, making me go on an earring hunt in this coming storm but I didn't think *this* was what she had in mind.

Atalie's eyes landed on mine, and they were broadcasting some serious nervous energy. "What was that?"

"That . . ." I spiked an eyebrow, equal parts amused and bewildered. "I'm pretty sure it was a setup."

"What? Why . . . would she get that idea?" Her eyes fled to the backs of Josiah and my mom as they continued to walk farther away, not even peeking back once.

"Not just my mother," I teased, enjoying the opportunity to banter with her at a time when my words were actually working. It would just be a moment and they'd break again, but I took advantage of the glitch and added, "It was pretty clear your son was in on that too."

"Remind me to ground him for life when he gets back." Her comment should have sounded like a joke, but her voice came out in breathless whisps, almost like she was suffering. I caught my bottom lip in my teeth and held my breath, knowing I was witnessing her vulnerability.

It had nothing to do with grounding Josiah.

It had everything to do with the way she kept looking at me.

She felt this weird thing too.

Earlier at the house today was too much to ignore. However, underneath what I thought was her want, I felt her resistance, because she always found a way to pull away. I didn't want to make her uncomfortable, but that left us both dancing around this thing—apparently, we weren't the only ones who saw it.

"I wouldn't be that hard on him." There was nothing cheeky about my comment when I went on, "He's not a bad kid." I slowly shrugged like it was helping to ease my words out. Oddly, I was grateful for my mom for setting up this opportunity to talk to Atalie. It's exactly what we needed, some time away from the house and work. Time to talk. I wasn't going to waste it. "I, ah . . . wouldn't mind taking a walk with you." I pointed to where Mother had asked us to look. "If you think that'd be okay?"

There was a mild twinkle in her eye that softened the potency from the whirlwind of emotions I could see she was unsuccessfully concealing. She nodded just once and together we took slow intentional strides toward the water. The movement served as the perfect transition I needed to fill in the awkward gap of words. When we'd walked a good distance, I saw her shoulders relax, and I didn't want to risk making her nervous again by getting too personal right away. "So." My words came out casually. "Tell me something about you I don't know."

"I'm really not that interesting," she rushed. "My life is Josiah and work."

"You must do something for fun." I was super impressed with myself for staying calm. It was so different than how I had felt earlier. Something about the timing—or maybe it was having Mom and Josiah on our side—but I relaxed, feeling like this was meant to be. "You can't work all the time?"

She let out a sigh that started as disgruntled but the tail end of it fizzled into something I swore was amusement. "Nope, just work. I have a real boss hole."

A surprised chuckle tumbled out of my mouth. "I deserve that." Caught off guard, I bit my lip about the boss comment because she had a few points she could easily use to back that up.

"Well." Her head tilted thoughtfully to the side, and the corners of her lips curled up. "I mean he isn't *always* terrible."

That's what I needed to see. Not her making fun of me, but her opening up. I pressed on, "Something besides work. Any hidden talents?"

"This is not what you want to hear," she said with a serious face, "but I can throw up on command."

"Right." I motioned to her stomach. "Your sensitive blood sugar thing."

"It's more than a sensitivity. It's literally a switch. I just have to think about it and it's done. It's a superpower."

"That could be . . . attractive—" I chuckled, as I failed to come up with an appropriate way to describe it.

"Useful," she cut in. "I mean, I've never had to *use* it, but I could imagine like say, a kidnapping situation where I need a spare second to escape—I would totally test it out."

"As you should." I nodded, suddenly feeling grateful I hadn't been on the receiving end of this talent.

"What about you?" Her eyes shined back at me with piqued interest. "Same question."

"Well, I can recognize any font immediately within seconds of seeing it."

Her nose wrinkled like she had failed to understand a punchline in a joke. "Don't you have something more embarrassing than that?"

"Um, I can solve a Rubik's cube in under a minute."

"Lame."

"Why is that lame?"

"Both of those things tell how good you are at something. Tell me something you're bad at." Her brows lowered toward me in a serious manner, but the smile on her lips was inviting in a way I felt all the way into my gut. We had come to the end of the beach and stood right on the water's edge. The tide was high from the winds and would have been a great distraction had I wanted one, but I didn't need a distraction.

I was ready to confront my feelings.

I was never good with words, but when I looked at her with the dissipating sun rays lighting her face, making her smile the most captivating thing I'd seen in a long time, I had a better idea than talking.

I took a step closer to her, dropping my eyes to her lips in the same manner she had done to me earlier today.

Total payback.

"Isn't that obvious?" My voice started to crack now, but it was mostly still functional.

"Not really." Her words stumbled out, but she didn't back away.

I paused, yielding in caution, not because *I* needed to, because I didn't. With Atalie there wasn't a need to be guarded. She had followed me to a swamp. Her loyalty was proven, and my heart was open. I waited to give her time to say something or hint I had read her code wrong, but she didn't.

That was clearly more code.

Inching forward another step, I made my intention clear with my body language. She reciprocated, taking a step closer too. I held my breath, all previous doubts I had melted away and I affixed my eyes on hers. Her gaze seemed to vibrate right through me, skittering along my spine all while my heart ramped up, thumping at Mach 20 speed. If my heart was beating as fast as it could, the rest of my body was moving in the slowest setting as I wanted to memorize this moment.

My fingers found her chin, and the pads of my fingers skated along her cheek like she was the most precious thing I'd ever touched. I lowered my face so close that when I inhaled, her scent consumed me. I brushed my lips against hers, knees buckling when they were met with her softness. Like static, my lips clung to hers, fueled only by a whisper of a breath so soft it was like an act of worship to taste her. My mind recoiled back to when she said *that if it's right, it hurts* because this *pained* in all the best ways. I was heading fast to a severe case of skintingles—*like shingles but far more serious and you only get it from kissing*—and I didn't want it to ever end.

She abruptly broke our entanglement by sealing it with the distinctive smack of a smooch and taking a giant step back. Just the mere sound of it sent another rush right to my chest. Our eyes locked and I was left standing there, wondering how in this spinning world of unexplainable phenomenon could our casual relationship escalate into a kiss like that.

I knew the answer.

I was clearly a genius.

I had fallen for her.

I fought for control of my faculties, wanting only to kiss her more, but I could tell by the way she grazed her fingers over her lips nervously, she had a hesitation. I didn't want to make her uneasy. So, I retreated, fumbling for words as I wasn't sure what to say. I definitely didn't want to apologize because I *wasn't* sorry. Maybe I owed her an explanation because I could see how it *might* have felt random to her.

I deadpanned. *This talking thing wasn't working for me!*

I willed my lips to curl into a grin that was so forced it had to look cheesy, then I blurted out, "Finally!" Like I had conquered Mount Everest after struggling with the last hundred feet for years.

She smirked, while still concealing her lips with her fingers, and echoed, "Finally?"

"That was way more challenging than it may have looked." I quickly pinned on, "The talking part. Not the kissing. The kissing part was easy." Then I held up my finger in analysis, and that is when my word vomit started. "Well, not easy like I do it *all the time* . . . more like easy because I felt it, ah . . . natural, um. But not like natural, because you're just here . . . more like it was *you*, and, I ah, just wanted to kiss you, I've been *waiting* to kiss you but . . . uh, not if you don't want to kiss me . . . so you *stopped*, and"—I put my hands in the center of my chest in gesture and continued—"so I stopped. . . and I'm just not sure what I'm saying. Talking is hard." Clenching my fingers into fists, I dug my nails hard into my hands, feeling the sting of being a world-class dork.

Reminiscent of a chaperone at a junior high dance, Mom's *too loud voice that was obviously warning she was coming* cut through the air. "We'd better get back before the weather gets even worse." My eyes swept away from Atalie to see Mom's smirk was as telling as Josiah's pink face when she said, "I just remembered I wasn't wearing earrings today."

"Oh, is that so?" I stated matter-of-factly while waiting for them to catch up to us. In a way, her timing was perfect, because although, I felt ready for this. . . *this* thing happening with Atalie. I sort of felt like I needed someone to do the talking for me for a while.

Talking was hard.

Kissing would be better.

TWENTY-TWO

Atalie

The next morning, I arrived at Trey's house steeped in apprehension over what had happened between us. Timidly I walked to Trey's office, feeling ready to talk about the kiss and how I had been feeling. It was the only way forward. My hands trembled as I peeked inside the room, but I could already tell by how dark it was that he wasn't there. Relieved—maybe disappointed—I turned on my heel to look upstairs, but I bumped into Mrs. Michael in the hall.

"Morning, Atalie, how are you?" She smiled at me fondly.

"I'm okay." I motioned to the dark room behind me. "Is Trey out for the day?"

"Oh no." She shook her head, adamantly. "He'll be right back. He ran out to meet Tonya for a—" Her voice dropped off so abruptly, the look on her face told me I wasn't the only one alarmed by her words. "It was a breakfast thing." She waved her hand in a dismissing way, almost like she was trying to take back her words, but it was too late. She rushed to add, "He had some stuff to give her."

I didn't need to hear an explanation. That was the second time this week Trey had seen Tonya. His actions were speaking loud and clear. They slammed the door to my heart, instantly shutting down all current and future feelings for Trey. It made sense. Deep down I knew Trey had always been Tonya's. *They'd been together since he was fifteen! Of course, he'd go back to her. I was a distraction while he waited for her.*

A stupid distraction.

He probably bought me my car to make her jealous.

I can't believe I didn't see it before.

"Oh." I swallowed hard, passing a giant pile of shame with my breath. I backed up a few steps, shifting my direction to aim towards the kitchen. "I'll get to work in the kitchen then."

She nodded, without saying anything, but the look on her face told me she was sorry.

I sped to the kitchen with one single goal in mind: *quit my job*. I had no idea what I was going to say, but I had a growing list of reasons. I didn't want to leave Trey in a bind, but the thing was, *this was an emergency.* Never more determined, I walked over to Josiah, who was sitting in his usual spot at the table, and asked, "Can I have a sheet of your notebook paper?"

"Sure." He flipped to the back of his spiral-bound book, tore out the first blank sheet, and slid it across the table. "Are you making a shopping list?"

"No." Pulling out the chair next to his, I plopped down next to him. "I'm writing a letter of resignation."

"What?" he said with a smile, anticipating a joke.

I kept my eyes low on the paper as I started to collect my thoughts. "It's hard to explain, but it will work out."

"Are we going home?" His voice was soft now, hinting of hope.

"Not yet. But I think we're getting close. I talked to the lawyers last night and they explained I'm going to have to cut my losses and move on. It doesn't make sense to not move forward. However"—I dropped my voice even more— "it's not for you to worry about."

"What are we going to do for money?"

"I'll figure something out. Summer is starting in a week. Maybe I'll open a smoothie stand on the beach."

His eyes rounded like he couldn't have heard anything more frightening. "Great, now we're for sure going to starve to death."

Biting my lip to avoid laughing at his pretty on-point joke, I picked up his pencil and wrote.

Mr. Michael,

This is my official letter of resignation. I'm sorry I can't offer you a two-week notice and my official last day is today. I won't be returning. Thank you for the job opportunity and good luck in all you do.

-Atalie

Without rereading it, I walked the letter down the hall and placed it in the center of his desk. Unshed tears pooled in my eyes, telling me to slow down. I didn't understand why I was crying. I certainly didn't love cleaning toilets. I also knew I wasn't scared about money. I had mostly got over the whole swamp encounter thing as well and wasn't holding a grudge about that. Now I was left with the memory of Trey kissing me like I had meant something—*no, everything*—to him.

That was *clearly* a mistake because he was still dating Tonya.

I had gotten caught up in a silly fantasy.

I needed to find a way to forget about him.

The fastest way was to put distance the size of a job resignation between us.

Stealing a tissue from the box on his shelf, I swiped several times over each eye, then dropped it into his empty trash can, gathered Josiah, and left.

Twenty-Three

Trey

I wouldn't say it was nice to see Tonya again, but it did give me a weird closure I hadn't realized I needed. We easily laughed with each other in a way we hadn't done in the better part of a year, as we could finally speak openly about our downfall. We talked for hours about everything like we used to. I came away from our breakfast seeing we were parting as friends—and would always support each other—but we were clearly moving fast in opposite directions. She admitted she had already gone on a couple of dates, and it didn't make me feel weird or jealous. If anything, it made me excited to think about . . . a possibility of dating.

Okay, the truth was, it made me think about Atalie.

I obviously didn't want to make her uncomfortable by asking her out if I didn't think she'd be willing, but she kissed me back. That meant something. I believed if I could spend some time with her *not at work*, we could get past this weird stage. Since I could be slightly awkward with this stuff, I formulated a plan to ask her out. I was going to walk up to her and say, "I see you like to breathe, as do I." If she laughed, I'd ask her if she wanted to breathe somewhere together over coffee. If she didn't laugh, I'd be more strategic and ask, "How does one successfully ask you out?"

It was the perfect plan.

In my humble opinion.

With my T-shirt flung over my arm, I carried my giant stuffed Yoda into his new home, eager to stow him safely on a shelf in my office. I wasn't materialistic, but my dad had given him to me and if my memory served me correctly, it was the final gift he had given me. He wasn't a nerd like me. He didn't understand the obsession with the series, but he had gone out of his way to have this stuffed animal—I mean action figure collector's item—signed by Frank Oz for my thirteenth birthday.

Best gift ever.

I will eternally love Yoda.

It turned out he was too big for my shelf, so he got an upgrade to the chair in the corner. I smoothed his authentic-looking, threadbare shawl and fluffed up his scantily scattered hair so he'd look handsome and wise. My mind shifted to Josiah and how he was also a fan of the series. My lips spread into a huge grin when I thought of how excited Josiah would be to see a Yoda this cool. Yoda would definitely be allowed in our new man club. Turning on my heel, my eyes caught a piece of loose-leaf paper on my desk. I was a clutterphobe in every sense of the word and hadn't left anything on my desk. I quickly snatched it up, taking in the thesis in one eye sweep.

Atalie quit.

Just like that.

Maybe she got a better offer?

I could make her an even better one.

I pulled out my phone, found her in my contacts, and pressed send. No answer. She was obviously avoiding me, but I had no idea why. Or maybe I did know why?

I kissed her.

It's the only thing that changed.

I needed to talk to her. Even though my throat was closing in at the thought of speaking actual words to her right now, I had to apologize. I didn't want to because I wasn't sorry but if that is what it took to make her feel comfortable, I would because I was unwilling to accept a resignation.

A resignation meant I was losing her.

I went to throw the stupid letter in the trash, but when I held it above the trashcan, I noticed a single soiled tissue resting on the bottom.

I didn't use a tissue.

Yoda didn't use a tissue.

Atalie was the only other person in here.

That *meant* there was only one person who'd use a tissue in my office.

I'll admit in every sense of the word, communication was hard for me, but this wasn't rocket science. Something I did made Atalie cry and quit so abruptly she couldn't even tell me to my face or give me a notice. I'd think if we could Crocodile Dundee together and survive that, she'd at least tell me what was going on to my face. There was only one thing . . . I had crossed a line.My stomach was all the way up in my throat right now, but I pushed through it, because I needed to find her.

I didn't waste a minute and I was in my car, heading south after entering the address I had gotten from her application into my GPS. My brow wrinkled as something about the address seemed so familiar. The weirdest thing too was it wasn't that far. My map showed it was a few blocks closer to the beach—which wasn't possible.

I must have typed in something wrong.

I doubled-checked the spelling, and everything seemed to be correct. I continued heading south, but as my GPS read my directions, I seemed to know instinctively every turn before it was even announced.

I'd driven this road before.

Actually, to be correct, I rode my bike on this route hundreds of times as a kid. Even though it had been years since, I remembered it like the pages of my favorite book. This was the road I used to take to visit Damion. His parents had lived about a mile from my parents' house, which was partly why we had become best friends. I wasn't prepared to think about him right now, so I focused on my GPS, waiting for it to steer me away, but it didn't. It hung tightly to the path I knew, stopping at the house *I knew.*

My breath hitched in my chest.

There's no way.

I had to have typed it in wrong.

Not only was this the address of Damion's childhood home, but it was also in a very expensive neighborhood, right on the beach. Atalie could never afford this house.

There was a mistake.

Or she lied on her application, and she didn't seem like the type to lie. So, it was clearly a mistake. I threw my car into park and hesitated, wondering if I should go knock when it was undoubtedly the wrong house, but I didn't have any better ideas, so I decided to take a chance. I knocked two times before a light flashed on in the darkened hall on the other side of the door. When the door opened, I had half expected to see Damion's mom, but it was Atalie. Her lips parted but stayed silent. "Atalie," I started, still amazed at the coincidence. "You'll never guess but I have the craziest story to tell you about this house."

Her eyes rounded, and her face paled. "How did you find me?"

"I looked in your employee file. I wasn't trying to be a crazy stalker, but I got your note," I blurted out, but my words couldn't slow as I continued, "I'm not okay. We need to talk about this. I'm guessing it's because I kissed you, and I felt I needed to apologize. I was also worried something bad happened," I rambled while motioning to her standing there looking freshly showered in pajamas with long cotton pants and matching cozy-looking shirt. Her long hair was piled high in one of those messy buns, but I thought she looked amazing. I fought every selfish inclination I had to just stare at her. If that kiss had affected how I felt about her, it had awakened me fully to see her for the amazing woman she was. "You look great. Clearly not dead or anything. Is everything okay?"

She dropped her voice. "Josiah's sleeping upstairs, but if you can be quiet, you can come in." She opened the door wider for me, and I passed through it, taking in the view from the inside. A lot of the interior had changed since I had last been in here, but some of it was similar.

Oddly, the sofa was the same.

I stood there, staring at the sofa like it was about to grow legs and put on a talent show. Before I had a chance to check my manners, I blurted out, "Atalie, how can you afford this house?"

Leaning her back against the wall, she crossed her arms. "It was my mother-in-law's house and my husband inherited it right before he died."

"Wait a second." My head started to swell with memories I didn't even know I had. My eyes fled to the stairs, where pictures lined the wall. Pictures in the same place as they were the last time I had been in this house. Pictures I'd seen before.

Damion and his parents.

Damion and his grandparents.

Damion on his graduation day.

Damion on his wedding day.

I had never made it to his wedding. They had a Midwestern wedding to be near her folks, and I had planned on flying in the day of, but Tonya's grandmother had passed the week prior, and perfect bad timing made her funeral land on Damion's big day. I had sworn to him I'd make it out another time, but I was always busy.

My brain had already solved the riddle.

My heart didn't believe it was true.

I took a long step closer to the wall to examine the photo of Damion and his bride.

Damion and Atalie.

His Atalie.

My Atalie.

He never called her that, though. I would have remembered a name like that. He called her . . .

I turned back, so panicked for clarity. Jerking my thumb over my shoulder toward the photo, I whispered, "Lea."

Her eyes filled with tears I couldn't identify. She wasn't happy. I don't think she was sad. Her weakened voice floated out. "What did you say?"

"That's my friend, Damion." I motioned to the photo again. "This was his house." I took another step toward her, feeling an immense sadness wash through me. "You're his Lea, right?"

"Nobody called me that but him." Her breath was shaky, like she had seen a ghost. "How did you know that?"

"Damion was my friend." It was a simple comment, but it carried a heavy emotional weight which immediately impacted us both.

"I don't believe it," she scoffed through narrowed eyes. "I'd have known you. He never once talked about his friend Trey."

I paced forward another step closer to her, still in disbelief about how I had missed so many details over the years. Suddenly I saw how everything wove together. I wasn't wrong about this. "Did he talk about his friend, DJ?"

She turned away from me, but I could see the despair budding in her eyes. "Stop it. I don't know how you know these things, but it's cruel to come over here and do this to me." She bawled her fingers into a fist, but even that didn't hide her trembling fingers. I fought every urge to reach out to her, to touch her, but I feared she'd scream because she looked so afraid.

"My real name is Demetrey. My middle name is James. When I was little, my friends called me DJ and that's how Damion knew me. When I started my own business, I thought it was more professional to use my real name.

However, that was such a long name, Tonya started to call me Trey and that stuck."

Atalie's hand fled to cover her mouth, and she spoke from behind her palm with barely audible words. "Say that again."

"Uh, when I was little, my friends called me DJ."

"Not that part."

"What part?"

"You're real name."

"My real name is Demetrey?" My words came out like a question as I wasn't sure what she was fixated on. Before I could offer another word about Damion, she pushed herself off the wall and fled into the kitchen, where she stopped at a little secretary desk in the corner. With focus, she frantically pulled the drawer open and tore through a stack of papers that looked like bills. She seemed to know an organization to the piles of papers, and when she found the right one, she flipped it open and stared at it for a few seconds. Then she raised her eyes back to me, but there was an unsettlement in them I had never seen. She crossed the kitchen again in urgent steps, stopping an arm's length in front of me, and flashed the letter before me. "Is this you?" she asked in an accusatory voice.

It was dark in the room as she had obviously been getting the house ready for bed, and I couldn't really see what it said, but my eyes glossed over it, and I got stuck on the letterhead.

My letterhead.

I yanked the letter from her, soaking up the words I had seen before.

There's no way.

I could never do that to her. Now it was my turn to shake my head, feeling like the floor was collapsing beneath me. I stammered back, "I had no idea."

Her pupils were sharp and cold; daggers would look more friendly. "Are you admitting that this is you?"

"Yes . . . but I had no idea."

My words came out in a rush, but she ignored them as she stormed toward the door, crying in a harsh whisper, "Get out of my house!"

I moved, but not toward the door. I had to make this better. I was pulled toward her, reaching out and placed a hand on her hip, wanting nothing more than to take it all back.

I didn't have a clue.

I would have never done it.

Lord, please I prayed. Take it back!

I didn't know.

Slapping my hand away, she yelled, "You are not welcome here! Don't you ever say Damion was your friend again. Friends don't do that." She went to open the door, but when she turned the knob, the door was jammed. "This stupid door always gets stuck." She leaned against the door and twisted the knob with two hands. "Give me a minute." She looked back at me and snarled like she was trying to keep this argument going. Then muttered under her breath, "Oh, for Pete's sake." Her annoyance at the door grew, and she gave it a swift kick and tried to turn the knob again, but it didn't work.

I stepped forward. "Here, let me try."

Her brow was furrowed but even through her anger, she looked stunning. "No, you can't help me. I'm trying to kick you out of my house!" she whisper-screamed.

"I can see what you are trying to do, but it's not working. I can help."

She relented, stepping back, letting her arms cross in front of her. I pressed on the door as hard as possible before turning the knob until I felt a release, and the door swung wide-open. I stood in the center of the threshold—one foot inside the house and the other foot on the porch. "It looks like the house shifted and you should get a new hole drilled. One that aligns with the knob. I could do it for you if you have a drill."

She glared at me.

"Or . . . you could say thank you for opening your door," I joked, but her nostrils flared, indicating she wasn't in the mood for jokes.

"You need to leave."

Right. We were fighting. I had hoped my impressive handyman skills would have made her forget about that. I lowered my voice and spoke softly, "I never meant to hurt you. I didn't even know about you. It was business."

"Business?" Her voice squeaked. "Really?"

"My accountants told me I needed to free up capital and recoup assets."

"Recoup assets? That's what you call it? That's hilarious," she mused with an angry scowl. "Because I call it being a heartless jerk."

"Let me explain—"

She cut me off, saying in a rush of words, "How about I explain to you how it felt to sell the house Damion and I built together. The house we brought Josiah home from the hospital to. The home we made!" There was a fire in her eyes as she held them in communion with mine. "Or how about I tell you how it felt to have to empty out my dead husband's art studio and hand it over to real estate developers. He spent a whole summer painting a mural on the outside brick wall, and in one second everything was leveled. Or the worst part, trying to explain to my son he can't go back to school or see his friends again because we had everything taken from us." She flung her hand wildly and went on. "Lucky for us, we had inherited this house and Damion hadn't had time to move it into his name yet, or you would have claimed that too. So, no, you don't get to explain!"

I wanted to die. This wasn't supposed to be like this. I hated myself for what I did. I couldn't walk away without telling her everything. It was the only way. "Atalie," I started, still unsure how I would explain my actions in a way that she understood because I agreed I was scum. "I promise you, I had no idea. Damion had unpaid loans from my company. He had needed money for the expansion, and the banks didn't want to finance him, so I gave him the money. He insisted on making it a loan, though, and I didn't care if I ever got the money back because he was my friend, but he was the one who insisted we have papers on the loan. I ensured he had a great deal and charged him zero interest."

"Oh." Atalie snorted through a fake laugh. "I'm sure you gave him a deal, all right."

"But his business was slow, and he didn't want to tell you, so instead of paying them back, he kept borrowing more money and before long, he had exceeded the worth of that building, so he put up both businesses as collateral. It got worse every year and his loan got out of hand. He never wanted you to worry. I honestly didn't care because I had the money to share. It's the truth when I say my accountants suggested I call in the unpaid loans. I had no idea his name was on the list. I never saw the list and I never thought to check." I motioned to the house before me. "This is all a shock to me right now. I thought it was people I didn't know, and—"

"Oh, let's feel sorry for the billionaire," she said sarcastically, letting her eyes dig into mine.

"Atalie, I had no idea you had to sell your home," I whispered.

"How could you not know? You took my businesses from me, so I had no way to pay for my house." She flung her hand toward me in an angry gesture. "For what? Gas for your private jet to fly around with Tonya?"

"It wasn't like that!" Fear was fueling my words now, and my voice ticked up a notch. "I was at a crossroads where I was looking at laying off a hundred of my best employees, and it made sense to call in money owed to me."

She sarcastically snapped her fingers right in my face. "Just like that."

"No, not like that."

"I don't understand. You said Damion was your friend. How could you not want to help his family?"

"After Damion died, I was a wreck," I started to pour my heart out in desperation to make her understand. "Forty-year-olds aren't supposed to have heart attacks. I couldn't fathom he was gone. I actually started to reach out to you many times to see if I could help, but I always froze because I was so broken. I didn't think you'd needed to hear me cry when you had suffered a bigger loss. I had no idea you were dealing with money issues, or I would have immediately." I shook my head as these memories burned, but she needed them, so I kept going, "I stopped caring about everything. I stopped going to work. Tonya and I started fighting all the time, and my business crashed. I was letting my team run my company for me, and I didn't double-check what loans were on the list and . . . I'm a jerk."

"You got the last part right."

"I'll fix it. I'll get your house back. *Please* let me make this better."

"I think you've done enough." She glared through scary eye slits, looking like she wanted to spit hot tar at me. "And to think I had actually started to *like* you, you stupid piece of garbage. No, you're just another billionaire who doesn't care about the little guy. I'm glad I quit today, or I would've never found this out. Could you imagine what would have happened if I didn't know this?"

It didn't *exactly* sound like a term of endearment the way she whispered-screamed at me, but there was something braided into her words that hinted she might have been considering . . . *something,* and that was what I clung to. "What would have happened?"

"Get lost!"

My heart released rapid-fire bullets that stung on impact, each getting lodged into my throat. *She felt it too.* "Atalie, what would have happened?"

Ignoring my question, she sputtered, "You don't get to break me anymore."

Suddenly I saw it clearly. Her tears weren't about her husband or losing everything. She was crying because of heartbreak.

New heartbreak.

Heartbreak *I* had caused.

Even in the shadows of the dimly lit room, the heartbreak was radiating from the depths of her eyes. Raising my hand, I reached the tips of my fingers out to caress the side of her cheek. Holding my breath, I waited for her to slap me, but instead her wounded eyes latched onto mine, seeking clarification. I was done explaining. I didn't want her to hurt anymore. Everything inside me said I had the power to fix my mistakes, and I needed to reassure her everything would get better. "I'm going to make it better," I whispered. "I promise."

It was as if my words threw her back to her reality, and she took a heart-stabbing step back and bit out, "I'm going to tell you again, and if you don't listen, I'm going to call the cops. You need to leave."

Some moments in life play out in slow motion, and you can count them out on your fingers how rarely they happen. For me, the day I heard about my dad's disappearance was one of them. The day I heard about Damion dying was another.

Right now. I was living in another one.

Bonding my eyes with hers, I begged her to forgive me. I didn't care if she understood. I was not sure if I understood at this point, but I needed her to be willing to forgive me because I was just as lost as she was. I'd put on a good show, trying to move forward but I had been broken for the last year, and clearly not thinking about a lot of stuff. Stuff I really messed up. However, right now, I knew it wasn't an accident that she came into my life. I could see her struggle to break my eye lock, but I leaned closer, pulling her back like there was an invisible string pulled tight between us, tying us together.

Because we are tied together.

There was no other way this story could happen unless we had been guided . . . somehow. "Atalie," I whispered, feeling her name burn in my chest. "Why did you apply for your job?"

"Ah, I needed a way to put food on the table since you stole my bank account."

"No." I reached forward, trying to grab her hand, but she pushed my hand away and gave me a warning look. I wasn't giving up until she saw it too. "It was Damion," I said softly. "There's no other way."

"Stop." Her voice was so weak, I felt bad pressing the issue, but I had to.

"It's the only thing that makes sense. We were both hurting. I majorly screwed up letting my team run my business for me, but I can fix it. I can totally get everything back for you and you can stop hurting because we can be there for each—"

"Get out of my house!"

I heard her demands, but I was affecting her, so I pushed on, "Atalie, I'll admit I suck at reading people, but you must admit something happened between us. I can't walk away from that—"

"Then I'll call the cops." She practically lunged over the couch to where her cell phone was sitting.

I knew she wasn't calling my bluff, and I didn't want any legal problems, so I held my hands up and called back to her, "I'm leaving." I even took steps until I was standing on her front porch. "But I'm going to fix this. I promise."

"Eat dirt, you disgusting jerk!" She scurried back to the door and tried to slam the door in my face, but it popped back open, leaving us facing each other. I was silent, but she called out, "Oh, not this stupid door again!" She slammed the door, but it floated back open. "Seriously!" She wrapped her fingers around the edge of the door, crying real tears. "Stupid door!"

"Here, let me try." I turned the knob the whole way and pulled the door as hard as I could until I felt it stick. Then I was left standing with the door in my face. So, I went home to work on my plan.

Twenty-Four

Atalie

I quickly locked the deadbolt and attached the chain, putting as much distance between us as possible. Then I turned, letting my back slam against the door so hard it hurt, but I wanted it to hurt because I needed a worse pain to shadow the anguish that burned in my veins. My knees buckled. My legs caved, and I slid down to a human ball of agony on the floor, where I violently wept. I warped into a weird trance where my mind kept tossing out random sentences Damion had said to me over the years. At the time, they seemed like casual conversations, but now they were strung together.

Lea, the bank won't take our loan, but I talked to my buddy from back home and he will invest with us. It's great news!

Babe, I know we need a new roof, but business has been slow.

I got the money for the roof.

Bad news, I think the leaky roof gave us mold. I don't have the money to fix it, so we will need to stay at your mom's.

Great news, I got the money to fix the mold!

I know you want to send Josiah to that expensive private school, but I don't think we can swing the tuition. Can we look at the public school down the street?

I have the best news! I got it figured out, and we can send him to St. Mary's!

Babe, the economy is shutting down and people aren't booking weddings or gatherings. Everything is closing. The state won't let us open.

Lea, it's been months since I've been able to host any events. I think we need to pull Josiah from school.

No, I can't ask for any more loans. The businesses can't handle it.

No, you don't need to get another job. Just focus on our family and help with the studio when you can. I don't want you to worry.

It's okay, he can stay at school.

It was gutting to relive all the clues. I couldn't deny they'd been there, and I felt like a monster. Damion had always made it clear he didn't want me to worry. I knew money was tight, but I had no idea he was borrowing money aside from the initial investment. Wishing desperately he had confided in me so we could have faced it together, I buried my face in my hands and released more tears. The sobs were rooted so deep they made my stomach wrench, and I had to press my palm firmly on my gut in support.

Flashing my eyes heavenward, I cried, *"I could have helped. I would have added more classes and booked more events. I could have taken a side job! Anything would have been better than to find out now you had been carrying this burden by yourself. This wasn't just your life to fix."*

The more the tears flowed, the more my anguish proliferated, setting even more tears to bloom in my suffering eyes. I sobbed for what felt like hours until I finally felt sorrow's hold on me weaken, and I let my final cry escape from my lips and whispered, *"At least you could have fixed the stupid door."*

Twenty-Five

Trey

It had been a week since I had learned how I had broken Atalie. Lucky for me, Robert had gotten back from his honeymoon and completed his on-boarding because I didn't have the heart to deal with business right now. My business had always been everything, but all I wanted to do was fix Atalie. I also wasn't stupid. I understood I couldn't *fix* her, but I was going to do what I could to make it better. I already extended an offer to the people who bought her house for double its value. They immediately accepted. As for the art studio, that was a little harder.

Okay, more than a little.

Impossible.

The properties had been leveled, and a hotel had been built in their place. I was trying to be creative and think outside the box, but I still had no clue how I was going to fix that. I could buy another building and put another art studio in it, but it wasn't about having an art studio as much as it was about having a piece of Damion. Then like a gift that floated down from heaven, a seed of an idea implanted into my mind, reminding me of something Damion had given me.

It had to work.

It was the only piece of Damion I had left.

I headed to the attic but paused at the top of the steps because I got that feeling you get when you enter a graveyard. Like you are about to traipse on sacred ground, and your body senses a need to be quiet and respectful. I took another step and let my hands fall on a rusty compass. Memories of Damion and me hiding under the stairs—pretending to be lost on a voyage with only my trusted compass to guide us—flooded my mind. A child's imagination—so pure and innocent—was always a magical thing. Doubting this hunk of junk even worked anymore because I had dropped it at least a hundred times, ran it over with my bike, and took it swimming in the bathtub, I flipped it over and watched the needle bounce until it rested on true north. Just for fun, I let my eyes follow its direction, leading me to *him*.

My purpose for coming here tonight.

The compass worked perfectly.

After my dad had disappeared, I stopped going to school. I would get up in the morning and get dressed and leave, hiding behind the bushes until after the bus had left the bus stop. Then I would walk down to the port and watch the waves while holding my breath, praying one of them would bring my dad home. It felt like that scene in *Braveheart* where that woman was tied to a post, waiting for a rescue, only to understand too late and there was no one coming, and she had to save herself. I had to save myself from my heartache. I didn't trust I could do it, and I vowed to never love someone enough for them to hurt me this badly. If I was going to be honest, fear of heartbreak was the main reason I had stayed with Tonya as long as I had. I loved her *enough,* but not enough she could break me.

When the school finally got a hold of my mom to let her know I hadn't been coming to school, instead of getting mad when I confessed what I had been up to, she started to join me. We spent a month at the port together—doing nothing more than healing—before she insisted it was time to go back to school. I was terrified to leave the port, thinking I would miss his return, but she insisted it was time.

The night before my return to school, Damion manifested on my doorstep, holding a canvas he had wrapped in his pillowcase as a makeshift backpack so he could carry it on his bike. He never said a word when he untied the twine, revealing the oil painting he had made for me.

He had an otherworldly talent that captured my heartache, transforming into an image of beautiful strength. An image of an abstract man kneeling with an extending hand, open in offering. Titled: Forever Bonded and signed with his name. It was an enormous gift to know he cared and took the time to try to understand what I was feeling. Still, I had this beautiful work of art that reminded me, even though my dad had passed, he would find a way to hold my hand and guide me.

Damion's kind heart and talent were like no other.

A better man than me in every way.

I understood so profoundly why Atalie suffered. I removed the painting from the wall, setting it on the table to prepare it to be moved. It wasn't an art studio, but I didn't have a doubt in my mind that this was better.

A piece of Damion holding her hand.

TWENTY-SIX

Atalie

I completed my after-dinner cleanup and was sorting through the unopened bills on my counter. I opened one envelope and felt the first hint of a real smile in weeks. "Look, Josiah." Holding up the piece of cardboard stock paper that was inside, I proudly stated, "It only took two weeks to get my certification from the state to be a Food Service Operator. I can open my smoothie stand."

"Joy." His voice came out in a flat, unamused tone. "Now I can plan how my bed will look on the sidewalk." He seemed to be at that age of youth where you leave behind the magic and wonder in everything you see and start to remove the filter to see true reality.

"It is joy because it means I can work again. Now all I need to find is a food truck I can afford, and we will be the dream team again." There was a double knock at the door, and my heart stopped. I only knew one person who was loyal to a double knock, and I didn't want to see him.

"Mom, someone knocked." Josiah half sat up from his position of holding down the couch. "Do you want me to get it?"

"No," I said, bitterly as I stuffed my certificate back in the envelope. "They can go away."

Another double knock.

"Mom, maybe it's someone important. Should I look out the window?"

"No, they might see you and they need to get the hint and leave."

I waited for a third double knock, but there was nothing. I paused, feet cemented to the floor, not daring to stir the air in case he might sense we were home. When I felt it was safe, I tiptoed to the window, and gasped at what I saw.

"What is it?" Josiah swooped in next to me, crawling behind the sheer curtain, pressing his upturned nose against the glass. "Wow, that's a lot of unicorns!" His voice came out hinting of awe as he took in the dozens of giant stuffed unicorns all aligned on the sidewalk. "What are they for?"

"Nothing." I pulled him away from the glass and straightened the curtain back to closed. I was about to grab the blanket from the sofa and throw that over the window too, just to spite Trey.

"How'd they get there?"

"Um, that's the thing about unicorns, they are magical." Scratching the back of my neck, I could feel a nervous heat turn on, and I rambled on, "And they just do that."

"Mom, they are not real." He motioned to the window. "Didn't you see they were stuffed?"

My eyes filled with tears, and in my head, I screamed at them. There was no way I wanted Josiah to see me cry, nor did I want him around that monster ever again. "Baby, can you go upstairs to shower?"

"No." His voice came out etched with his stubborn independent thing he had going on recently. "I want to see the unicorns."

"You can't go outside right now. It's dark, and we don't know who put them there. We can look at them in the morning."

The look he shot me was one of disappointment, but he was obedient and left to go upstairs. Having zero intentions of seeing Trey ever again in my life, I picked up my phone and texted him.

Me: *Get off my property or I will call the cops.*

Trey: *I have something for you.*

Me: *I don't want your stupid toys.*

Trey: *Something else. Something you would want.*

Me: *Get Lost!*

Trey: *Keys to your home. And the deed. Everything in your name.*

A tortured groan fell from my lips.

He said *home.*

Not house.

I didn't want anything from him, but *my home*... that was mine to begin with.

I deserved those keys, but I didn't want to see him. I knew his game. He was obviously trying to lure me to him so he could talk, but that wasn't happening. He didn't deserve that.

Me: *Leave them on the step and get off my property.*

Trey: *Done.*

It had to be a trick. There was no way he was going to let me off that easily. I waited a good five minutes until I cracked open my front door, eyes landing on a single key centered on a manilla envelope. My hands were already trembling as I reached forward to grab them, but what I saw next *slayed* me.

Propped up against the supporting beam of my deck was a beautiful canvas of a man reaching out his hand. Though I had not seen this image before, its style was *forever etched in my heart.* Dropping to my knees, tears flowed freely. I didn't fight crying as I reached forward and placed the tips of my fingers on the palm of the hand. It was beautiful imagery which awoke a feeling of warmth and sentiment in my heart that only opened the dam to my tears even more.

I forgot about the key.

I forgot about the ridiculous unicorn parade on my sidewalk.

I forgot about Trey, who was still lurking in the shadows.

All I saw was my husband reaching out from the heavens and holding me one more time.

It was like my prayers to change the rules of time had been answered.

And somehow, I was able to steal one more moment.

I didn't know it before, but I clearly understood answered prayers had a way of altering your perception and healing the most severed hearts. I no longer saw Damion as being departed. He was here with me, holding me. A beautiful gift no heart was big enough to even capture. My heart swelled and overflowed with so much happiness, reminding me of the joy Damion had been to me and the joy he would want for me.

I could have stayed in the moment forever—in my own bending of time—but a creak from behind me slammed me out of ecstasy. I didn't need to turn around to see who it was, and I wasn't ready to look at him, but he brought me this gift, and I had to know more. "How did you find it?" I asked through a sniffle while keeping my eyes locked on the painting.

"Damion made it for me after my dad disappeared. It was always special to me, but he's telling me it's your turn to have it."

Not wanting to cry in front of him, I clamped my palm over my mouth, and pressed hard to silence even the tiniest squeaks. I truly believed Trey one thousand percent when he said he heard Damion say to give this to me.

It's so perfect.

So beautiful.

So Damion.

I nodded through my stifled cries and, as best as I could, and peeped out, "Thank you."

I couldn't wait to show it to Josiah. We'd treasure it forever. That reminded me Josiah had to be getting out of the shower and I didn't want him to find me missing. I got up from my knees and swiped my sleeve across my eyes. "I gotta go in. Josiah's in there."

"Do you want me to bring it inside for you?" Even though he offered, his feet didn't budge forward as they remained respectfully planted at a safe distance behind me. I narrowed my eyes, ready to spit insults, but when I locked eyes with him, my breath pulled in hard.

He was crying too.

Crying with me.

Crying with Damion.

Though his memories were different, I could see his pain manifest in his eyes, which was no different than mine. It was clear to me we were kindred spirits brought together by the soul we were both missing. In the gentlest kiss of the wind, I swore I heard Damion's baritone whisper. "Just let him in."

Like finally seeing a sign point north on a foggy street under a charcoal sky, I nodded. Damion had given me permission to let Trey bring the painting into my house, where we could hang it in a place of honor. I knew those words had a double meaning, with the latter meaning being the one of greater urgency. Damion was giving me permission to let Trey into my life.

Into my heart.

He was giving me permission to chase the kind of joy I didn't think I could allow myself anymore.

Bigger yet, he was giving me permission to love again.

I finally understood that moving on *wasn't* forgetting.

Squeezing my house key in one hand, the feeling which ran through my chest was pure bittersweet. As nice as *home* sounded, I could not go back there. Sure, we'd go back to visit, but I had grown so much in the last year. Other than a house, there wasn't anything else for me to go *back* to. Seeing what Trey had done for me, and everything else he'd done to help Josiah, he was giving me more of a feeling of coming home. Only it didn't stop there.

It never stopped there.

The affection I had for Trey—which I had previously suppressed and padlocked, even lied to myself about its existence—was bursting out of my heart, pleading with me that it was time to admit my true feelings about him. I ran my tongue slowly over my bottom lip, distinguishing the sting of dryness. Then I held out my hand to Trey in Damion's example. "You can come inside."

His eyes fastened on my extended hand, but he didn't move. He gently ran his top teeth along his lip in a curious manner before latching his eyes back onto mine. "Are you sure?"

Smiling sweetly while budding light tears, unable to control the whirlwind of emotions that were spiraling through me, I nodded and replied softly, "Yes."

His lips spread into an affirming smile that sent another rush of emotions through me, ringing out the breath in my chest giving me a I'm-dying-but-in-a-good-way sensation. Seamlessly, he latched my hand, letting his fingers braid into mine and with his other hand he effortlessly scooped up the painting, and followed me inside.

I knew without a doubt that this was meant to be. Just as I had known Damion and I were made to love each other; I knew that Trey was part of the plan too. That was how I knew I was *Maid for My Billionaire Boss.*

One year later

Trey's beautiful eyes of infinity sparkles shined back at me. He flexed his fingers, squeezing my hands one more time while his chest moved up and down, dividing each of his deep measured breaths. My life couldn't be any more perfect. Like in a fairy tale, Trey lowered his face while holding his eyes locked with mine and said, "I do."

Happy tears hooded my eyes and threatened my perfectly applied three coats of mascara. Blinking them back, I let out a slow breath when I heard, "I now pronounce you man and wife. You may kiss your bride."

Trey gave me my favorite look. The one I refer to as his heart-stopper, as it had a tinge of boyish grin blended with his adoring eyes. My lips parted for him in a kiss which felt sweet yet promised everything . . .. but short because people were watching. Our small audience broke out into applause. We ended our kiss with our arms still locked and we followed our small wedding party of just Robert and his wife down the aisle. We were met with showers of confetti like nothing I had ever seen. The strands were long and straight. Reaching up, I pulled one from my veil, studying it before feeling my lips spread into a reminiscing smile. "This is shredder paper, isn't it?"

Trey's perfect white teeth peeked out from his mischievous grin. "I had to. It was too perfect." Wrapping his arm all the way around my waist, he pulled me closer, and we raced to evade the attack of the shredder paper.

It was so beautiful.

So perfect.

So . . .Trey.

The End.

Thank you for reading Maid for My Billionaire Boss!

About J.P. Sterling

Becoming an author was clearly an accident. Writing was cheaper than therapy, and after my first book hit number one on the Amazon charts, I developed a writing addiction.

Aside from writing, I'm also a wife and homeschooling mom, a holistic nutritionist, a jewelry designer, a professional archivist, former college instructor and lover of all things dark chocolate.

Author Clean Code: I like to make my stories about the story and not about a bunch of profanity, mature content, or graphic violence that are only there to shock you. I write my stories to be family friendly.

If you'd like to subscribe to my free newsletter to be the first to hear about new releases, please click the link. https://landing.mailerlite.com/webforms/landing/q9c0v3

For free audio books please visit:

https://www.youtube.com/c/JpSterling

Find me social media:

https://www.facebook.com/jpsterlingauthor

https://www.bookbub.com/authors/j-p-sterling

https://www.instagram.com/authorjpsterling/

https://www.tiktok.com/@authorjpsterling

Acknowledgments

I am terrible at these things because I always miss people and I feel I need to start off with an apology to the amazing people I will forget—SORRY!

THANK YOU to my amazing readers! You are the only reason I continue to write and I love it so much when you reach out to me on social media. Please, don't hesitate to tag me, follow me and let me know you are here. I really would not be doing this without you.

THANK YOU to my amazing husband! He has never read my books and I doubt he will read this, but he is the rock who supports my dream in other ways.

THANK YOU to my amazing team of beta readers, editors, and proofreaders. I have to add a huge shout out to the entire team of My Funny Valentine authors who I worked with for a year to launch this book.

THANK YOU to that person who I call my developmental editor. You really are so much more than that. My books would be sludge without you.

Also By J.P. Sterling

Falling for the Boss Series

Maid for my Billioniare Boss

Upcycling my HillBilly Boss (Coming June 6, 2023)

A Heart that Dances Series

Dancing on Broken Ankles

The Stars We See

A Heart that Dances

A Heart that Loves

Water and Stone Duet

Ruby in the Water

Lily in the Stone

Christmas in Amesbury

Halidaze in Amesburry (Coming Christmas 2023)

Amaryllis Farms

Cowboys and Princesses (Date TBA)

CPSIA information can be obtained
at www.ICGtesting.com
Printed in the USA
BVHW032322090223
658265BV00025B/528